Lightning Killer

Wes Overland

GW00502871

A Black Horse Western

ROBERT HALE · LONDON

© Vic J. Hanson 1950, 2003
First hardcover edition 2003
Originally published in paperback as
Blue Lightnin'! by V. Joseph Hanson

ISBN 0 7090 7263 5

Robert Hale Limited
Clerkenwell House
Clerkenwell Green
London EC1R 0HT

Typeset by
Derek Doyle & Associates, Liverpool.
Printed and bound in Great Britain by
Antony Rowe Limited, Wiltshire

ONE

Glaring lights, blaring noise. The raucous voices of men, the shrill ones of women. The clankety-clank of a rocking piano, the squeaky bleat of a concertina, the twang of a guitar. The click of the balls in the roulette-wheels, the decisive voices of the dealers calling for bids. The polyglot crowd. Cowhands, teamsters, prospectors, gamblers, miners; men who lived by their wits and men who lived by their hands. Drawling, happy-go-lucky rannies with guns at their hips and a good time in their eyes. Swedes, Mexicans, half-breeds, Indians, a few Chinese and Negroes . . .

Tucson, Arizona, on a Saturday night. It's largest saloon, the Golden Wheel, with its long semi-circular bar, its ornate mirrors around the walls, its stage, its dance-floor, its gambling layouts.

Tonight was a big night. A thousand head of cattle milled in the corrals down at the stockyards. There were cowboys in town from as far south as San Antonio. Lambs for the fleecing . . .

All sorts and conditions of men. Good, bad and indifferent men . . . Men out to enjoy themselves. Laughing men. Singing men. Men with women. Men with friends.

Against a wall one young man, unsmiling, alone. A slim young man dressed all in black, a single heavy gun low at his hips, a wide brimmed sombrero shielding his eyes from the light. His clean shaven face was smooth, almost boyish, except that the high-bridged nose, wide thin mouth and long chin gave it a slightly predatory look. The skin was the colour of smooth light leather, the eyes beneath the hat-brim seemed very dark, the long hair curling from there was black, it shone a little in the light.

The young man leaned against the wall, his back flat to it, his thumbs hooked in his belt, his legs crossed a little. A cigarette hung from a corner of his tight lips. The smoke from it curled slowly upwards. The young man squinted against it and, now and then, raised a negligent hand to brush it aside.

Men looked covertly at him as they passed. Because he was alone, because he was unsmiling and, it seemed, not drinking. He looked a mean young cuss. Probably just another of Craig Jepson's gunslingers they figured. He was standing right next to the black door marked Private. From there he could survey the whole room. And nobody could get behind him. To the right of him the staircase angled upwards. He could see all of that, too, until it vanished into the dusky upper regions.

Past the bottom of the stairs the bar began. At the other end of this was the small dais where the musicians congregated. Then came the stage with its dusty red curtains.

The night was well under way and merry withal, when a big man came from between the aforesaid curtains and stood on the narrow strip of planking before them. He raised his hands and bawled:

'Your atten-cheeun, folks!'

Big Bill was the barker of the Golden Wheel and when his bull-like roar shook the rafters people stopped to listen. A hush fell on the packed motley company.

'As a special attraction for you to-night Mister Craig Jepson is proud to present Miss Annabella Strudel and her troupe of young ladies . . . Thank you.' Big Bill bowed ponderously and left the boards amid a storm of clapping.

The pianist, concertina-player and guitarist, augmented now by a man with a kettledrum and another with a washboard, struck up a border-ditty as the red curtains slowly parted. A bevy of young females in spangles and tights pranced on to the stage and began to sing and kick their legs around. The crowd went wild and the painted percentage-girls found themselves taking back seats as their swains left them and moved nearer to the stage. Gaming was suspended and the shirt-sleeved dealers shrugged their shoulders philosophically and began to pile together their winnings. Their time would come again before the night was out.

A lean man with two low-slung guns, carrying a black valise came through the door marked Private and began to go around the tables and collect the cash. He filled his valise then he made again for the back door. The young man leaning against the wall beside it was grinning now and, in common with everybody else, clapping his hands to the beat of the music. He yelled with the rest as the star of the troupe, Miss Annabella Strudel, came on to the stage. She was red-haired and pretty, shapely and vivacious. The man with the valise turned to have a look at her too before opening the door behind him. He was still feasting his eyes on this vision of femininity as he sidled through the door.

It was doubtful whether he had really noticed the young man. He had his back to him now. He did not see him move. Maybe he only sensed his movement, with a sense, gone for a second while he watched the women, returning suddenly. A sense that went with the lean alert look of him, the low-slung guns, to one of which one of his hands suddenly moved. His hand stopped, clawed above the walnut butt, as something hard and unmistakable was jabbed into his ribs. A strange hand came beneath his own and lifted his gun. His other hand was powerless, holding the valise.

A voice said: 'Move,' and he was jabbed again.

He went through the door and the young man followed and it closed behind them.

'Keep moving,' he said.

They went along the carpeted passage to another door marked Private. The lean gunman lifted a fist and knocked. A voice said: 'Come in.'

The gun jabbed again. 'Go on,' said the other voice, softly, menacing.

The man with the valise opened the door, moved in. 'I've got the cash, boss,' he said.

The man behind the desk rose, his hands in view.

'Stay like that, Craig,' said the young man, kicking the door to behind him, moving away from the man with the valise, covering them both.

Craig Jepson had not gotten to where he was by taking chances. He froze.

'What the hell,' he said. 'Who are you?'

His voice was taut. He was the nervy, scheming type. Thin. Prematurely-greying hair.

'Don't you remember me, Craig?' said the young man. The other's eyes widened a little, recognition flashing into them, astonishment too.

'Johnny Salom! What brings you back here? When did you get out?'

'Few weeks ago. Good conduct.' Johnny Salom laughed suddenly. It was a harsh brittle sound, tearing at the taut air, making it quiver. 'Good conduct! Me! Can you imagine that? What brings me back here. . . ? You should know what brings me back, Craig. You should know.' The staccato speech died, then spluttered again as he jerked his head at the gunman. 'Put that valise on the edge of the desk here. Near to me. Take it easy, pardner . . .' The voice became soft. 'Easy.'

The gunman did as he was told. His lean body was tense, his eyes, as he watched Salom, were dark and droop-lidded.

The young man took the valise. 'Back up,' he said. 'Back up.' He backed himself towards the other door, the one that led through into the alley. He let the valise fall to the floor. He watched the other man, moving away, halting, a wide stretch of floor between them now. He held his gun steady. His dark eyes beneath the wide brim of the sombrero were impersonal, black. The eyes of a killer.

He reached behind him with his free hand and turned the knob of the door. He edged it open. He bent and picked up the valise and his eyes, shuttling swiftly from one to the other of the two men, seemed suddenly mocking.

'You won't get away with this, Johnny,' said Craig Jepson.

Johnny straightened. With a swift movement he holstered his gun, let his hand dangle free. His other one was weighted by the valise.

'All right,' he said. 'Stop me. Go on – stop me.'

The other gunman, a professional with one gun left to him, a man deadsure of his own prowess, seemed graven by astonishment for a moment. Then he let his body fall slackly forward, his eyes on Johnny Salom.

'You pore damn fool,' he said.

He moved then, faster than seemed possible. The air was torn with movement, then it was full of powder-smoke, the reverberations of a heavy gun.

Craig Jepson moved too, nervily swift, sudden panic in his heart. Then he screamed as his gun was spun from his grasp. Blood spurted through his fingers as he grasped the tattered pulp of his hand. The room was spinning around him, the spreadeagled figure of the gunman on the floor seemed to be floating up to meet him. From afar he heard a voice say:

'Remember me, Craig. Remember me.'

Then he slumped forward over his desk in a dead faint.

10

2

Johnny Salom holstered his gun as he went through the door, across the back porch and through the frame door into the alley. He paused for a moment, getting his eyes accustomed to the darkness, then he moved forward swiftly. He stopped, flattened his body against the wall. His gun glinted as he drew it once more. It was an action as swift as spitting, and as natural.

The faint glow that was the mouth of the alley was darkened by men's forms: one – two – three. Three men who were not at the concert, who were maybe making their way there when they heard the shots. Shots that would not have been heard by those inside with the singing and the noise. The hundred to one chance.

Johnny Salom turned, moved along the wall, passed the door he had just quitted. There were no shouts as he moved into the deeper darkness, only the hurrying footsteps. They had not seen him. But up ahead was a dead end. A fence which would only serve to silhouette his figure if he climbed it.

He opened another door and passed through into an empty hallway, a dusty staircase angling from it. The backstairs, used sometimes by residents who wanted to go out without passing through the bar-room.

The stairs creaked a little beneath his tread as he began to climb them. He had holstered his gun but his hand swung near the butt of it. The black bag, disregarded now, hung heavy at the end of his other arm. He reached the landing and as he did so heard movements in the nearest room on his right.

He turned the handle of the left-hand door. It was locked.

He moved along to the next one. It opened and he passed inside. He was closing the door gently when the one across the passage opened; closed; footsteps thudded, fading as they went down the stairs.

He closed the door completely, turning, knowing by the peace of his senses that the room was empty.

He leaned against the door, his eyes probing the darkness, noting the shapes and positions of the pieces of furniture between him and the grey square of the window. Then, swaying his body in his high-heeled riding boots he minced swiftly across the room. From the window, hidden behind the fold of a curtain he could see into the alley.

At first it was like looking into a pit of blackness, then, gradually, the walls began to appear to him, the dull shine of the uneven ground. Further down, by the backdoor to Craig Jepson's office, two men lurked. He figured the others were inside. One – two maybe more. And pretty soon the balloon would go up and they would be having reinforcements. Why hadn't he made a break for it, blasted his way through while he had a chance? And had a pack on his heels pronto? No, that wasn't the way . . . But neither was this the way. Skulking in a hotel bedroom with the buzzards massing below and the occupants of the room liable to pop in any minute.

He wondered who was the occupant of the room. He sniffed: there was a faint perfume in the air . . . To cap it all, it seemed like he was in a woman's room . . . Women were poison. . . ! So were lynch ropes! Yeh, maybe he had ought to have made a break for it . . .

He shrugged suddenly and began to move away from the window. Then he heard the cries from below, the sound of running feet. The sounds spreading until they were right below him, mingling with and finally killing the fainter sounds of the music and the singing. With one stride he crossed to the window again. The alley was empty.

He retraced his steps across the room. Then he stopped, stiffening, his gun leaping to his hand. Footsteps were echoing along the landing. He skirted a small table in the gloom, brushed against the coverlet of the bed and passed through a curtain into the little washroom.

There was something about the dragging slower pace of those footsteps that told him they were coming to this room. He knew his hunch was correct as they stopped and he heard the door open. The footsteps became sharp again. The sharp, clackety-clack of a woman's heels.

The man behind the curtains heard the scratch of a Lucifer, then light filtered through to him. His gun was in his hand as he peered through the narrow parting of the curtains.

The girl had her back to him. She wore a purple silk dressing-robe. The wealth of her red hair gleamed beneath the light. As he watched she undid the sash of the robe and slipped the garment from her shoulders. She was clad in a spangled costume which ended at her thighs in ruffled tights. Her long shapely legs were encased in white silk stockings. Her shoes were red, high-heeled with pompoms.

She half-turned before she sat down on the bed and Johnny Salom felt a queer jerk inside of him as he saw her profile. What that jerk meant he did not know. He only knew with his limited knowledge of women that this one was very good-looking. Like a gay doll she had looked on the stage. But there was nothing doll-like about the soft but firm lines of that chin, the set of those lips, the cheeks bronzed but with no artificial colouring.

He recognized her as Miss Annabella Strudel, leader of the dancing troupe. Women he despised. Dancing women he thought a lot of fakers. The sudden feeling that had startled him died as quickly as it had come as the girl turned her face away and bent over as she sat on the bed.

She straightened, putting her white silk stockings on the bed beside her. Despite himself he discovered that he could not take his eyes off her back, the lines of it as she moved, the soft womanly contours of it.

She rose and began to do something with the top of her costume. She paused, transfixed in a listening attitude as steps thudded along the passage.

'Miss Strudel!' called a man's voice, then the footsteps stopped and somebody rapped her door loudly.

'Yes?' she said. Her voice was clear, a little husky.

'Miss Strudel. There's bin a shootin'. There's a chance the guy who done it might still be around. All the girls are down stairs. The boss 'ud like you to come

14

down as well if yuh would . . .'

The girl seemed to hesitate for a moment. Then she said:

'All right. I'll come down.'

'You ain't seen nobody have you, Miss Strudel?'

'No, I haven't seen anybody. Carry on, I'll be down in a minute.'

'The boss said I was to wait – if you don't mind, Miss Strudel. I'll be just along the passage.'

The girl gave a little shrug.

The footsteps started up again. The sound receded a little, then stopped. The girl sat down on the bed and drew on her stockings once more, put on her shoes. Then she rose and donned her dressing-robe. She blew out the lamp.

The man behind the curtains heard her cross the room, heard her fumbling a little. There was a chinking sound before that of the opening door. Then after the door banged shut the man heard a key turn in the lock.

He heard her footsteps going down the passage, heard her speak; then their footsteps started up together and slowly faded away.

He came out from behind the curtains and crossed to the door. He leaned his weight against it and pushed. It creaked a little but would not budge. It was made of stout logs and the lock was large and heavy.

Johnny Salom drew his gun.

TWO

He stood immobile, the weapon in his hand, while seconds ticked by. Then with a little shrug he returned it to its holster. He turned on his heels and crossed to the window. He looked out.

Noise was intensified beneath him now; all around him. He heard thudding footsteps on the stairs along the passage. Somebody was shouting but he could not hear the words. He disregarded the sounds behind him. The locked door was between him and them. A door they would not try because it was Miss Annabella Strudel's room and she had just quitted it.

By contrast with the hullaballoo which seemed to shake the whole building the alley seemed quiet. But, as his eyes pierced the gloom, he realised that there were a couple of men on guard down there. One was almost directly below the window. The other was leaning against the backdoor to Jepson's office.

The window was half open. A breath of cool air came through it. The subtle scent of mesquite, and desert dust tickled the nostrils of Johnny Salom. A breath of freedom.

The man directly below began to pace slowly. His beat was before the stairs door. There was a glint of a gun in his hand as he moved.

The man up at the window stood motionless, only his eyes shining a little in their sockets as he watched the moving man.

The saloon was a hive of sound. A voice in the passage bawled, 'Aw, hell, he's miles away by now.'

Another one replied, '1 told yuh. We heard the shots. He'd have had to get past us to get away. He must be around someplace . . .'

'We'll have to bust all the doors open,' said another. The net was closing in; the scent of freedom was pungent. There was only one break in the net – and he'd maybe get himself tangled up in it. He had to take that chance.

He eased the window gently higher. What little sound it made was killed by the din the jackasses were making. He only hoped the man below did not glance up and see it move.

Johnny Salom put his legs through the window first. Then he was sitting on the sill. This was the crucial moment. The guard below was still moving slowly. The one further along the alley was still. Only grains of a second trickled by in time but they seemed like hours to Johnny Salom.

The man below moved nearer then obligingly paused directly below.

He heard something swish and he twisted. He did not have time to look upwards before the heavy weight hit him, blanketing his vision and bearing him to the ground all at the same time. Cold steel descended with crashing force on the back of his head and he knew no more.

His pard heard the sound, an undefinable one and tried to pierce the blackness with his eyes. Nearer the ground, where the outside lights did not penetrate all was woolly vagueness. He moved forward a little. Then he hissed: 'Skip.'

A voice answered him, woolly like the darkness, the wards unintelligible. He heard the scratch of a lucifer, then the glow of a partially shielded flame. He caught a glimpse of Skip's hat, his shadowy figure foreshortened against the wall. Then the flame died, was replaced by the red pin-point of a cigarette.

The man said hoarsely: 'The boss said no smoking.'

Skip's voice grumbled back at him. The man shrugged and went closer. 'Lend me yuh makings,' he said.

The dim figure by the wall slid a little closer. Then it moved with tigerish swiftness and the guard's mouth opened with shock. The cry that bubbled there was never uttered as a gun-barrel laid his temple open and sent him tumbling a dead weight to the dust.

Johnny Salom took off Skip's hat and replaced it by his own. Gun in hand, he catfooted swiftly along the alley. He reached the top, took off his hat once more and peered around the corner.

There was a line of horses at the hitching rack, his own paint pony among them. But there were men there too, spaced along the boardwalk. Others seemed to be ranging both sides of the street; it was alive with people.

And they didn't seem to be making as much noise as the jackasses inside . . . Johnny Salom moved back into the deeper darkness as two men passed the mouth of the alley.

He shrugged slightly and turned and went back along the alley. It was empty now except for the two unconscious men. He passed them. He had already forgotten them. He reached the tall wooden fence at the bottom and began to climb.

His progress was slow because of the valise he carried. The short hairs at the back of his neck prickled and his spine was taut as a bow-string. One of those two doors behind might be opened, a window up above, people on the main drag might take it into their heads to investigate up here. His body trembled a little as it was poised on the top of the fence. Then he jumped.

He landed on the other side on his haunches, bouncing like a cat. From that position he sprang forward and began to run. Before he had gone far he realised that there were a few people around the back here too. Maybe only drunken cowhands, and percentage girls taking advantage of the shindig to do some sharp business. He hugged the shadows and slowed down a little.

Even so, he almost blundered into a couple. The man broke away, moving forward swiftly, his hand dipping. The running figure did not pause in its stride, steel flashing dully in its rising and falling hand. The cowboy moaned and went down. The woman screamed shrilly.

With that scream ringing in his ears, Johnny Salom killed the urge to return and still it forever and ran on.

It seemed to him that heavy boots were thudding behind him but when he stopped the sound stopped too. Maybe it was the beating of his own heart, the killing frenzy in his own heart. The thin scream piercing it.

He was running parallel with the main drag and suddenly he rounded a dark outhouse and reached the end of it. Behind him the thin screaming had stopped but there were other voices, shouts, running feet now that could not be mistaken.

As he turned the corner a gun boomed back there. Already the jackasses were shooting. He felt nothing near him.

What happened next was sudden, unpremeditated, forced upon him by circumstances, yet acted upon immediately, with ice-cold nerves and a perfect muscular co-ordination.

A horseman rode down the main drag, saw the lean figure come around the corner. Leaned forward, peering at it then, with a shout, went for his gun.

Johnny Salom fired from the hip and the rider yelled again, falling backwards from the saddle, over his horse's tail, hitting the ground with a dull thud. The horse reared and bounded forward, shied away from the thing speeding out at it from the shadows. The man caught its bridle, swung back, vaulted into the saddle. The feel of a body on its back again, legs clasping its flanks seemed to give the beast a new exhilaration. It snorted and bounded forward. It settled almost immediately into a swift, smooth gallop.

There was a spatter of shots, spent bullets moaned

near. Johnny Salom turned in the saddle and thumbed the hammer of his gun, spacing the shots, moving the muzzle of the gun slightly each time. From his lips came a shrill drawnout yell, the echo of it following the echo of his shots, the sound of a man crying out, 'Oh, oh, oh,' in pain: the whole blending in a garbled jeer of derision.

The trail was before him, a good horse beneath him, a savage, triumphant exultation in his heart. The first blow had been struck. Others would fall – faster and faster until the man at whom they were directed was torn to ribbons, his punishment finished, all who belonged to him finished . . . dead, finished . . .

Behind him hooves clattered, thudded, settled into a steadily increasing drumming. Again Johnny Salom let out that piercing yell, unleashing from the tightness of his lips the rage and exultation that was like frothing bile within him. Bile collected there through years of silence and bitterness and rancour. Silence broken now, bile fermenting . . . murder . . .

The folks behind saw him silhouetted for a moment against the purple skyline and then he disappeared. Horse and rider were swallowed by the night and, in their turn, the posse followed it. The darkness seemed to get more woolly, peopled by fantastic things, as they plunged into the badlands.

2

Craig Jepson reclined in a plush armchair in the sitting-room of his private apartment above the Golden

21

Wheel. His wounded hand was bandaged heavily and held up to his chest by a black sling. He was in shirt-sleeves. His grey fancy vest, adorned with small pink feur de lis, was open, revealing the flawless white front of the shirt with its little ruff down the centre, open at the neck, the two ends of a black shoe-string bow dangled across it. His long thin legs were encased in black pipestem trousers, crumpled a little below the knees through being crammed into the tops of riding boots, bare now, a pair of leather moccasins on Jepson's grey-stockinged feet.

His gunbelt was thrown carelessly on the table but the gun from it was on the corner, at his elbow. He grasped the gun as his door was rapped.

'The marshal's here, boss,' said a gruff voice.

'All right. Tell him to come in.'

There was a pause then the door was rapped again. It opened and the man who came through had to stoop a little to do so. He straightened again, taking a few long steps to face Jepson. His age, like the saloon-owner's, was indeterminate. The seamed hard face, the impersonal greyness of the narrow sun-squinted eyes, the hair sprinkled with the same colour, the thick mousy moustache, the slight sag to the huge body – they could have belonged to an old thirty-six, or a youngish fifty.

Jepson took out a pack of cheroots. 'Well, marshal?' he said. The marshal took off his battered Stetson.

He turned his body and sat down stolidly on a creaking wooden chair. He said, in a deep impersonal voice:

'We chased him plumb into the badlands an' then we lost him . . .'

'You lost him?'

'That's what I said,' replied the marshal imperturbably.

Jepson jerked forward, held out the pack of cheroots. The officer took one and said 'thanks.' He reached in the pocket of his grease-stained vest and produced a lucifer. He cracked it expertly on his thumbnail and it blossomed into flame. He shoved his foot beneath the rail of his chair and jerked it forward, holding the flame in his cupped hands, out to Jepson. The saloon-man lit his cheroot, nodded, then threw his head back and inhaled. His movements were nervy, too quick for comfort. The lawman lit up himself and gave a few lusty puffs. Then he took the cheroot from his mouth and looked at it.

'These are good, Mr Jepson,' he said.

'Yes,' said Jepson. 'Yes . . . Tell me, marshal – how did you lose him?'

'Wal, I guess he had a fast hoss. Also he seemed to know the territory purty well – either that or he was takin' an awful lot of chances. He just seemed to vanish – out in the badlands there. Among the scrub an' the cacti an' them big queer-shaped rocks. We rode on for a bit. Then we ran smack-dab into a bunch o' Yaqui Injuns . . .'

'Yaquis?'

'Yeh. They thought we was attacking 'em. I had to talk fast to cool the chief down. A hornery ol' cuss. They hadn't seen no white-man riding. They was just

23

on the point of making camp . . .'

'Did you question 'em properly? Have a good look at 'em?'

'What – in the dark? – Dadblast me, Mr Jepson, all Injuns look alike – even in the daylight. As for questioning 'em – I couldn't get a word in edgeways with the way thet ol' coot was gabbling. I guess he was kind of questioning me – only, not being well up in the lingo, an' with him talkin' so fast, I didn't understand much o' what he said . . .'

'They're as cunning as foxes. They might've been shielding Salom. You ought to've brought one of them in for questioning . . .'

'An' started the whole pack of them at our heels like a boiling of devils from hell? No, sir. The Yaquis are friendly Injuns, they don't give us no trouble if we leave 'em alone: I aim to keep it that way.'

Craig Jepson leaned back in his chair and blew smoke down his nostrils. The cheroot seemed to be soothing his nerves. He said:

'Marshal Cuthbertson, how long have you been in this territory?'

The big man's eyes were almost closed as he squinted through a haze of blue smoke. He said:

'I've been here two years, Mr Jepson. I thought mebbe you'd remember that.'

'I'm a man who has a lot of worries, Marshal. My memory is good but it is not infallible.'

The lawman inclined his head gravely in understanding. Jepson went on:

'You have not been here long enough to remember

Johnny Salom. His mother was Kate Salom, who lived in that lopsided log-cabin at the back end of town, down by the creek. She was found drowned two years or more ago – I guess that would be just before you came. Johnny was her only son. Nobody knows who his father was. Some desperado from over the border most probably. Johnny's certainly got mixed blood in him. He was always a bad one. Even when he was a kid he kept getting into scrapes. The old marshal, Peters, who went just before you came, clapped him in jail many a night to cool him off. It seemed like the boy hated Tucson and everybody in it – except maybe his mother, and you couldn't even be sure of his feeling for her. He had jobs and lost 'em. Fights, insults, thieving. Pretty soon nobody would keep him on. His mother worked for me a bit. She was a mighty hand-some woman and I guess there was something about her that made men fight over her. She wouldn't hear no harm said about her boy. I had to ask her to leave my place – she was like a kind of a jinx. After that it seemed like she got to hate the town as much as her boy did. She shut herself up in her cabin and would only entertain men from out of town . . .'

'I've heard some of the story,' said Cuthbertson, 'from different people. Different versions, too, I guess. The men f'rinstance – some of them say Dark Kate, as they called her, was an angel. Others, that she was little better than a man-teasing whore. The women – wal, they're pretty vehement on the latter point.' A guarded smile flickered beneath the marshal's thick moustache. 'I've heard a bit of mention of her son. What did happen to him?'

25

'Well, I guess he got tired of having his mother keep him. He vanished for months on end. He was seen in town only infrequently, sometimes dressed fairly well, sometimes down and out – everybody figured he was running with a wild bunch. Then travelling folks from time to time said they had seen a white kid riding around with a bunch of Yaqui Indians. There became little doubt later that the kid was Johnny Salom, but whether he was actually living with the Indians or just hobnobbing with them nobody knew. If only the latter he was certainly doing something that very few white men have done.'

Cuthbertson nodded sagely. 'Yeh,' he said.

Jepson nodded with him. 'Even you, marshal, a comparative stranger to the region know that the Yaquis, although not as warlike as many of the larger Indian nations, will have nothing to do with palefaces. Although they will let white people pass them unmolested it is dangerous for anyone to presume on their seeming friendliness and try to penetrate into their villages. They have secret rites and codes. Any Yaqui who turns to the white men's way of life, as so many other tribes are trying to do lately, is, if caught, tortured to death . . .'

The marshal nodded again sagely, thinking meanwhile that Craig Jepson could certainly spiel mighty pretty when he put his mind to it. Almost like a schoolmaster he was, sitting back in his armchair, smoking like a lord, and waggling a finger to illustrate his points. Mighty interesting points, too, for all that.

'The Yaquis never were a big Indian nation like the

Sioux or the Blackfeet. Mebbe that's why they never went on the warpath in force. Bands of 'em went wild from time to time, stuck up a traveller, robbed a store or two, derailed a train – they still do tricks like that, as you know, the same as white men do . . .'

'My job'd be a bed o' feathers if the only trouble I had was from Yaquis,' said Cuthbertson.

'Just so . . . But in the times I'm talking about there were more Yaquis in this territory and they weren't so docile. Well organized bands of 'em broke out from time to time and raised hell. People said they were being incited and led by a white man. Some said Johnny Salom. Others pooh-poohed the idea. What could a kid like him do? He just frisked around with a lot of Yaqui bucks because the white folks of Tucson wouldn't have nothing to do with him. Me – I don't know. He still came into town, spoke to nobody and what was more unusual, interfered with nobody. People left him alone. If he preferred Indians he was welcome to 'em. Everyone began to refer to him as the Yaqui Kid . . .' Jepson paused and selected another cheroot. His talking seemed to have made him steadier. He handed the pack to the marshal and with a murmured 'thanks' the big man took one. They lit up.

'And then what happened?' said Cuthbertson.

Jepson took his cheroot from his mouth and studied it. 'Well,' he said. 'Then the Kid shot two men – prospectors called Trim and Bullocks. Killed them both. He said he hadn't shot 'em of course. But he was tried and sentenced to fifteen years in the penitentiary.

27

He got off lightly I guess. His youth did it. He was only eighteen then . . .'

'An' now he's out?'

'Yes, after twelve years. He must have behaved himself plenty to get away with the other three.' Jepson's voice became lower, almost as if he was speaking to himself. 'He'd be about thirty now. He doesn't look it . . . Yet – I didn't recognize him at first. He doesn't seem a lot older but he's changed in another way.' His voice rose, became brittle as he looked straight at the marshal. 'He's a killer. A wild beast with added intelligence and training. He's got to be stopped. This territory won't be safe until he is stopped . . . Why, Joe Crickmore was my fastest gunslinger – but he never had a chance. Salom beat him to the draw – shot him clean between the eyes . . .'

The marshal looked down at the white mummified hand in the saloon-man's lap. 'He beat the two of yuh,' he said. 'He must be a marvel to be able to do that . . .'

'I had to get my gun out of a drawer,' said Jepson shortly.

THREE

The silence languished for a bit. The saloon-owner seemed to be brooding.

Finally Cuthbertson said: 'Those two prospectors who got killed – did they have anything to do with the mine?'

'The Horseshoe Mine? No, a bunch of men who worked for me found that afterwards . . .'

The marshal's lips curled again under his moustache. 'Quite a find, too.'

'Yes,' said Jepson. 'But its petering out now. It'll be closed soon.'

'Yuh don't say.' The marshal wagged his head sagely. 'Still, no good thing lasts forever . . .'

'Right now I'm not concerned with the mine,' said Jepson.

'I know,' said Cuthbertson, 'neither am I . . . Don't you worry, Mr Jepson, we'll get that scallywag. He gave us the slip tonight but first thing tomorrow I'm gonna have half-a-dozen posses out scouring the badlands. Without grub and water he'd hardly ride far. I'll put a

29

prize on his head, that'll make the bounty-hunters sniff:
one of 'em'll get him sooner or later . . .' The marshal
rose to his immense height and clapped his Stetson on
his head. 'I'll be going,' he said abruptly and turned
and made for the door. 'So-long.'

He received a muttered 'good-night' from the
saloon-owner. Then he closed the door and lumbered
up the passage, past the hard-faced guard with the
drawn gun on his knees, past the other one on the
stairs. Jepson was not taking any chances. Still, after
what had happened to him last night, who would?

Back in the room the lawman had just quitted, Craig
Jepson lifted the mummified white hand in its black
sling and looked at it. There was a sudden sickness in
his dark eyes. Beneath those white folds was a bloody
pulp of tattered flesh and splintered bones. The doc
said if he wasn't careful he might have to have it ampu-
tated. It would never be any good anymore. His good
right hand. His gun hand. The hand he used to deal
with.

It began to tremble as he held it there. A spasm of
pain crossed his face and he let the mummified thing
drop into its sling. He sat on in his chair with the smoking cheroot held laxly in his left hand and stared with
dark unseeing eyes at the opposite wall. His lips were
twisted queerly, deepening the lines in the thin face
beneath the greying hair.

Marshal Lafe Cuthbertson acknowledged salutations on
all sides as he passed through the bar and along the
street. The Golden Wheel, after allowing the disgrun-

tled posse-men a few drinks, was closing up. People were wending their way homewards. With a few of them the marshal exchanged a word or two, enjoining them not to forget to get up early in the morning.

He moved on down the street and slowed down finally outside the narrow door and double blacked-over windows of the office of the Tucson *Herald*. He thumped on the right-hand window with his fist, just on the faded U of the stencilled name, which had many of its letters missing entirely. His manoeuvre had the desired effect. The window was directly below the room occupied by editor Jeb Downs and the sound echoed up there like the beat of a brass-drum. The upstairs window was flung violently open and Jeb stuck his head out, a woolly skullcap atop of it.

'Dadblast it!' he said. 'What in Tarnation d'yuh want. I've only jest got into bed. Cain't it wait till in the morning.'

Cuthbertson looked up. 'Sorry, Jeb,' he said. 'It's mighty important. Could yuh come on down for a minute?'

'Oh, it's the law is it?' said the editor. 'All right, I guess I'd better. Dadblast yuh, Lafe, all the same.'

The marshal chuckled deep in his throat as the window banged. He waited until Jeb bustled through the office, slung aside bolt and chain and flung open the door. Then he marched in saying:

'This is law business, Jeb Downs, an' I don't want no tantrums.'

'You'll damwell get 'em!' said Jeb, who had a voluminous greatcoat over his nightgown. 'What d'yuh want?

31

C'mon. I ain't got all night.'

He lit the lamp above his littered desk.

'Gimme a pencil an' a large sheet of paper,' said the marshal.

With a splutter and a flourish the little fat man, his bald head concealed by his skull-cap, produced them.

The marshal began to print in block capitals upon the white paper while the little printer watched him. At length the latter said in a voice that was surprisingly quiet now. 'You're bein' a bit drastic ain't yuh, Lafe?'

'It's called for!'

'Is it? What did the kid steal? A few hundred dollars, a drop in a bowl to Craig Jepson . . .'

'He killed a man.'

'Joe Crickmore deserved killing. He'd've been killed ages ago only nobody could beat him to the draw. He's killed himself – for that boss of his. He just got paid out in kind, that's all. It was a fair fight – even Jepson admitted that didn't he?'

'He smashed Jepson's hand. He laid three men out. Cal Morris's forehead's laid wide open. He might not live . . .'

'Jepson ought to've had his hand chopped off years ago. He's dealt many a card off the bottom of the deck with it – though I guess now he's so rich and almighty he wouldn't choose to think about them days . . . As to the others – wal, I guess you're right. They hadn't done the kid any harm. I hope Cal Morris gets well, no-good though he is . . . But I still think you're being too drastic. Nobody's been actually "murdered" yet . . .'

'The kid murdered before . . .'

'If he did I guess he paid for it. I guess he never had much chance to be anything else than a lobo wolf. His mother bein' a no-good like she was an' him never knowin' his father. Folks looking down on him ever since he was a shaver. No wonder he hated Tucson an' everybody in it. I guess they never gave him or his ma much of a chance. She was bad I guess – but I never heard of her doin' anybody any real harm . . .'

The marshal looked up at him, opening his mouth as if to speak, and the little man plunged on, his eyes snapping a little in the light.

'Yeh, I knew her. I knew her well. I ain't got no kith or kin. I do as I please. But I didn't lie with her of nights and ignore her and her kid by day as if they were dirt beneath my feet. Her an' her kid were welcome here anytime they liked an' they knew it . . .'

'What actually did happen to the woman?' Cuthbertson's deep voice cut in on his friend's tirade.

Jeb softened down. 'They found her one morning with her head in the creek at the back of her house. It was shallow, she wouldn't have drowned if she fell in. It was put down as suicide – 'cos of Johnny. She didn't seem the type to take her own life but – well, I guess she was powerful fond o' that boy . . .'

'He came out of jail. He'd got a chance to start afresh. There are plenty of places in the West where a man can get a job an' no questions asked. Why did he come back here? . . . answer me that,' said the marshal.

'I confess that's somep'n I cain't do,' said Jeb Downs.

Cuthbertson made a last decisive full-stop on the manuscript and flung the pencil down.

'There,' he said. 'Print me that!'

Jeb shrugged his fat shoulders. 'You're the law.'

'I want about a couple of dozen for early to-morrow mornin'.'

'I don't set up type for that kind of job to print any less than a batch of fifty. Wouldn't be worth my while. I'll do yuh fifty an' charge yuh the usual rates.'

'All right. Do me fifty, you damned ol' buzzard,' said the marshal. He was spinning on his heels as he spoke. He marched from the office, slamming the door behind him with a force that rattled the glass in the double windows.

Jeb Downs sighed heavily, picked up the pencilled sheet of paper and took it to a darker part of the room. There he turned on the light over the type-cases, picked up his setting-stick and started in on composing the job right away.

Just as he had promised the marshal was at the office early in the morning. Not so very long after dawn in fact.

The press was already running and Jeb himself was feeding-in the last of the white sheets.

'Where's Cracker?' said Cuthbertson.

'He don't start till seven thirty,' replied the fat printer drily. 'Anyway, I thought I'd prepare these for yuh with my own lily-white hands.'

'That's mighty kind of yuh, Jeb,' said the marshal, matching his friend's tone with his own.

'That's it,' said the printer as he snatched the last ink-wet sheet from off the moving platen. He picked up the whole bundle and shoved them into the marshal's arms. 'Here y'are. Mind yuh don't smudge 'em.'

'Thanks. How about the bill?'

'Don't worry. You'll get it. An' a bit extra on account of it bein' a rush-job and workin' of awkward hours. I'm a master-printer not an apprentice like Cracker. My rates are higher.'

'Make yuh damned bill as high as you like,' said the marshal, turning to go. 'I'll pay it.'

When Jeb spoke again his voice had lost its flippancy. He said:

'It's the kind of job I don't like, Lafe.'

The marshal did not turn around. 'D'yuh think it's one I do?' he said brusquely. He strode swiftly from the shop, but this time he closed the door more gently behind him.

As he strode down the street, although the hour was early people were already coming out all around. As he passed the stables horses were pawing as men groomed them and saddled them. The marshal walked away from the bulk of it all, answering shouted 'good mornings' with sober nods as he went along.

He stopped outside the door of his own office, which was part of the squat brick-built jailhouse, and inserted the key in the lock. He opened the door, went in, leaving it ajar behind him. A few seconds later he came out, carrying a hammer and a little bag, as well as the sheaf of bills. He locked the door behind him.

He was watched by a few people as he took a few steps sideways to the wooden notice-board which was pegged into the red-bricked wall. A man detached himself from the group and went across to him.

'Mornin' Marshal,' he said.

'Mornin', Inch. Here – hold these.'

The man took the bills, held them, reading them with a little pursing of his lips, as the marshal delved in his little bag for tacks.

Inch was still reading, moving his head slowly from side to side, his pursed lips fluttering, when the marshal nudged him. Then he handed over one of the bills and the lawman tacked it up.

By this time the rest of the folks had formed a half-circle on the edge of the boardwalk. They waited till Inch Lemmings and the marshal had moved away then they crowded forward to read the notice. One of them pushed a lanky freckle-faced youth to the forefront saying, 'Here, Cracker, you're a scholar. Read it out to us.'

But Cracker Johnson, apprentice to Jeb Downs, editor and printer-in-chief of the Tucson *Herald*, had already read it over the heads of the others. He squirmed away. 'Read the durn thing yuhselves, yuh rubbernecked coyotes,' he said and loped off down the street.

They did not bother to follow and wreak vengeance on the youth for his impertinence. At the moment they were too engrossed, each in his own way, in deciphering the wording on the bill.

Jeb Downs, for reasons best known to himself, had printed a lot of it in old English capitals, which did not make for early morning reading with eyes that were sore with sleep and heavy with the effects of last night's binge. The notice in plain terse English, despite the printer's vagaries, was finally deciphered by all as conveying the following message. It was all too familiar to most of them and each digested it in his own particular way:

500 DOLLARS WILL BE PAID TO ANYONE CAPTURING, OR GIVING INFORMATION LEADING TO THE CAPTURE OF JOHNNY SALOM
(sometimes known as 'The Yaqui Kid').

HIS DESCRIPTION IS AS FOLLOWS:

They read the description. Most of them there had known Johnny Salom; many of them had known his mother, buxom, desirable Dark Kate. This description had points in it that reminded them of the Johnny they had known, yet some things that they did not remember about him, some things that almost seemed to describe Kate herself. It was a good description, if true: the marshal had made a first-class job of it.

But it was his postscript that was the real eye-opener; yet as they read it, they could not but admit that it was characteristic of Lafe Cuthbertson. It ran thus:

Anyone bringing in the carcase of this man, with his back full of bullets, will receive his just reward at the end of the rope.

That was a smack in the eye for unscrupulous bounty-hunters – though many folks affirmed that the damned Yaqui Kid deserved nothing better than a slug in the back for returning to the scene of his boyhood depredations and raising Cain once more. The kid was a menace: he ought to have been stifled at birth. Thus spake the bulk of the townsfolk. But there were others there, a shifting flotsam. Miners, teamsters, cowboys from the Lone Star State, strangers who were singularly unbiased, who spoke open admiration for the slick way in which the kid had pulled off last night's job and set the whole pack of them by the heels. He had broken the rules of the herd and it was inevitable that he should be hunted down. But he must be given the same chances any other hunted animal was given: a clean break and no shooting until they saw the whites of his eyes.

FOUR

The marshal passed down the street with his trusty assistant, Inch Lemmings. The latter's stocky blockiness was dwarfed by the lawman's height and wide shoulders. Inch had to hop a little to keep up with the other's strides. The marshal walked as if there was nobody else around, his head stuck forward a little on his thick neck, his jaw squared, his moustache bristling. To the greetings he received he gave curt nods – while Inch, with little friendly bobs of his ruddy head said, 'howdy Cal,' 'howdy Jim,' and so on.

At intervals the two men paused to tack up a bill; then passed on, leaving a buzzing group behind them. At length they reached the Golden Wheel, and tacked up a couple of bills there.

'I guess that'll be all for today, Inch,' said Cuthbertson. 'We've got something else to get on with.'

'We gonna ride now, Marshal?'

'Yeh.' The big man turned to face the people who were moving in on him. 'Is everybody ready?' he shouted.

There were cries of 'Yessir,' 'Sure thing,' 'Let's go get him.'

'Get yuh hosses an' gather out in front here then,' said Cuthbertson. 'Come on, Inch. We'll park the rest o' these bills and get our own nags.'

Ten minutes later a packed yelling cavalcade swept out of Tucson. The dust swirled behind them and settled at last in the deserted main drag as the horsemen rode into the growing heat-haze over the plains – spreading, rising, assuming a coppery tinge over the edge of the badlands.

A trio of dogs who had yapped at the heels of the horses in the van of the cavalcade frisked back to find fresh diversion in town, and the old men, women and children who had come out onto the stoops to watch the exodus went about their business and play. A lean Texan, one of those who had come with the trail-herd from San Antonio, leaned against the hitching rack of the Golden Wheel. Behind him, in the shade, two of his pardners sprawled. The lean man spat into the settling dust. He turned to the others and said:

'Woollies. Durn wild woollies.'

'Yeh,' said another. 'If they keep that up they'll frighten even the gophers outa their holes – they oughta sent a gink out with a big drum in the fust place to let that Yaqui Kid know they wuz comin'.'

'There ain't no gophers in this part o' the country, Perce,' said his somnolent neighbour.

'Who cares?' said Perce.

The somnolent one ignored this sarcasm and went on with a spoken reverie of his own.

'That marshal don't 'zactly seem no jackass to me.'

'If he ain't he wants to put a gag on some o' the members o' that posse of his'n,' said the lean man. He turned and crossed the boardwalk to the batwings of the saloon. 'I wonder if thet pesky bartender's woken up yet. Cain't seem to get a drink before noon without beggin' and prayin' for it. This is a Godforsaken country.'

His two pardners climbed to their feet and followed him. One of them spoke vindictively.

'I hope thet dern posse chases the Yaqui Kid plumb into Mexico an' then don't ketch him. An' I hope when they get back all the liquor's run dry.'

'If it's left tuh you it'll be supped dry,' his companion told him.

The lean one had reached the deserted bar. He thumped on it with his fist and yelled:

'Look alive, yuh squint-eyed, knock-kneed son of a seacow. Let's have some service in this yere rat-trap . . .'

The cry echoed through the buildings and out into the street. It was dying, thin, when it reached the rider whose horse's legs were buried in long grass on the little used approach to the north of the town. He reined in and listened. The sound died; the buildings at which he looked were like silent mirages in the morning haze.

The horseman kneed his mount forward once more, changing his direction a little. He dismounted finally at the back of a tumbledown barn and tethered the beast at a stump there. He unhooked a coiled riata from the saddle pommel. He patted the horse on its glossy neck with his free hand then, with the riata swinging at his side, began to walk.

He was a little ungainly on his high-heeled boots but

41

he walked lightly, like a cat with a burr under its tail. He moved along the 'backs,' among the outhouses, seeking the shadows, his black clothes blending with them.

He halted finally at the back of the livery-stables, among the bales of straw and the accumulated horsey rubbish of years. Wending his way catlike among the litter he approached the back door of the stableman's living-quarters.

He reached the door, lifted the latch, passed inside. Through the kitchen and living-room he went and into the wooden cubicle with the wide window that looked out into the stables.

He could hear somebody whistling tunelessly and finally he espied the bulging back of a man protruding from one of the stalls. The black-clad man opened the door of the office and passed out, his feet making no sound on the straw-bestrewed dirt floor.

He was behind the man, who was bulky, his whistling taking on a little gasp as he bent to rub-down the fetlocks of his charge.

He twisted his head a little and saw the legs of the man behind him. His whistling died and he began to rise, turning as he did so. He straightened out; a stocky, paunchy half-breed, and looked at the gun in the other's hand.

His startled sloe-eyes travelled upwards to the expressionless dark young face and he gasped:

'*Madre de Dios.* The Keed . . . The Yaqui Keed . . .'

'Hello, *amigo*.' Johnny Salom's voice was flat; it held no greeting, no promise. 'Where's ol' Josh?' he asked.

The half-breed's hands fluttered level with his shoulders. 'Josh? He ees dead.'

Johnny Salom raised his eyebrows above the dark smoky eyes. 'Dead? Since when?'

'T'ree months ago . . . He was a very old man . . .' The man's voice changed. 'Plees, Keed, what you want? I have . . .'

'All right. Stow it. I'm not gonna hurt yuh. Unless you try to pull anythin' . . . Who's boss here now?'

'I am, *señor*. Since Josh die. Eet ees my leetle place now. But times are hard . . .'

Johnny Salom twitched his gun. 'Stow it I said. All I want is my paint pony. The one I left in town last night. I figure it must've bin brought here. Was it. . . ? Don't try an' lie to me, you heathen. Was it?'

The half-breed's head bobbed around like an apple on a string. Finally it began to nod pretty regularly but the sloe-eyes were startled and shifty.

'Where is it? I'm attached to that pony, *amigo*. If anything's happened to it somebody's gonna pay. Where is it?'

The half-breed's hands fluttered. 'He ees not here *señor*. Ees not my fault. Mees Strudel she like heem – she borrow him.' The sloe-eyes rolled in agitation.

'The dancing girl,' said Johnny Salom softly. He reached forward with the hand that held the gun and placed the cold barrel lengthways across the other man's throat, forcing his head back. The man gurgled, his eyes, crossed now with the effort of looking at his assailant, were full of terrified pleading.

'Lend my horse to a dancin' woman would yuh?' said the Yaqui Kid. 'You'd better talk fast now, *amigo*, if you

43

want to save your neck . . . Where'd she take him? I want a quick answer an' a straight one.'

'She only went out five – ten minutes ago. She ride down to the creek every morning. I guess that where she go now . . . Eees true, *señor* . . . I no lie to you.' The half-breed's bulk quivered like jelly.

'All right.' Johnny Salom took his gun away from the man's throat and hefted it. The other's face went almost green; stark terror shone in his eyes as he cringed. There was a cruel light in the dark eyes in the smooth devil's face which seemed to swim now before the liveryman's gaze . . .

'All right,' said the emotionless voice and the lifted gun dropped a fraction. 'Turn around.'

The half-breed leaned his blubbery weight against the post of the stall as he turned around. In a terrified whisper that burbled in his throat but was hardly audible he called on all his saints to save him.

'Put yar hands behind yuh.'

Again the man did as he was told. The expected blow did not fall and the feel of a rope biting cruelly into his wrists was almost sweet. This devil with the smooth face was going to spare him.

He was lugged to the back of the stall and fell willingly on the straw beneath the speculative gaze of the horse he had been grooming. He submitted to having his ankles lashed and a dirty rag stuffed into his mouth and tied with a piece of rawhide. As he watched the dark-clad devil's legs until they vanished he called on all his saints to protect the lovely lady who had taken the paint pony.

2

The bartender ran in from the back of the saloon and confronted the lean Texan and his two pardners. His eyes were startled and he was panting a little.

' 'Bout time you showed up,' said the Texan, 'where we came . . . Hey! what's bitin' you?' This as the bartender turned and grabbed a rifle which was leaning against the whiskey-shelves.

All three Texans drew their guns with a swiftness which spoke of their continued skill. The bartender looked more startled than ever as for the first time he seemed to get them in focus.

He babbled: 'The Yaqui Kid! He's back!'

'Oh,' said the lean man. He lowered his gun. 'You pullin' our legs, pardner?'

'Whadyuh think I fetched this for?' The bartender tapped the rifle.

Followed by his two friends the lean man lifted the trap of the bar. The three of them passed through.

'Lead the way, pardner.'

The bartender looked uncertain for a moment then he turned on his heels.

He led the way into the kitchen and stopped before the window. With his rifle held ready he peered through. The other three craned their necks behind him.

At length the barman said: 'I cain't see him now.'

'You've bin seein' a bogey, pardner,' said the lean Texan.

'I tell yuh it was him. I could tell him. I useter know him as a kid . . .'

45

'They say he's changed . . . Nobody recognized him the other night.'

'He wore them black clothes like last night . . . Yeh, an' he was ridin' Cal Finnegan's horse what he stole . . .'

'Mebbe we'd better go out an' look then. Lead the way, pardner.' The lean man jabbed the barman playfully with his gun. The latter quivered and led the way.

They passed out among the ashcans. The barman, the barrel of his rifle pointing out in front of him, bent his flabby body almost double and peered like a mole.

Suddenly he started back. 'Look out, yuh clumsy coot,' said the lean Texan who was right behind him.

'Back in the kitchen,' said the barman. 'He's comin' back . . .'

'The nerve o' the galoot! Get back in boys an' let's see what he's aiming to do.'

They went back into the kitchen and congregated at the window. Johnny Salom came into view. He was not hurrying.

'He's still got Cal Finnegan's hoss,' said the barman. 'Damn him. Who's he think he is?'

The lean Texan chuckled. 'Ridin' around here like he owned the place while there's posses after him clean into Mexico . . .'

The bartender cursed again and raised his rifle. He put it to his shoulder, cradled his cheek, and drew a bead on the moving figure.

'This is where he stops ownin' anything,' he said. His finger whitened on the trigger.

A hand grasped the rifle and jerked it roughly out of

46

his grasp. Curses bubbled from the barman's lips once more and he turned furiously. The lean Texan held the rifle. His other hand went back then swung. The back of it hit the bartender flush in the mouth knocking him back into a shelf. A row of saucepans fell down with a hellish clatter.

One of the lean man's pards said: 'That's made the Kid stop an' look . . . He cain't see us here though.'

The lean man said: 'I ain't gonna stand by an' see a man bushwhacked without a chance . . .'

The others agreed with him in no uncertain manner. The barman looked from one to the other of them with hate-filled eyes. A little trickle of blood ran from his mouth down his chin.

'The kid's movin' again,' said the look-out.

'We'll move, too,' said the lean man. He turned to the bartender. 'Keep from under my feet in future, pardner. I don't like you. If I haveta hit yuh again I promise yuh it'll be with the barrel of a gun . . .'

'You can't push me around . . .'

'No?' The Texan's blue eyes were very bleak. 'Maybe you'd like tuh strap a gun belt across that belly o' yourn an' carry this on someplace else.'

Before the menace in the other's eyes the barman lost his bluster. 'I'm no gunfighter,' he said.

'So . . . Wal, don't get any ideas about gettin' back at me any other way. I've got enough rannies here right now to take this place apart.' The Texan hefted the rifle in his hand.

'We'll take this with us jest in case. Come on, boys.'

FIVE

Annabella Strudel sat on the edge of the creek and dangled her bare feet in the water. Her head was bare and the wealth of her shimmering red hair was tied demurely at the back of her neck with a black ribbon. Her head was protected from the steadily-growing heat of the sun by the shade from the small bunch of cotton-woods which were almost immediately behind her. But the rays of the sun shimmered on the water in which her feet were immersed, bringing a pleasant warmth.

She looked down at the sun-motes, dancing and sparkling, and wriggled her feet, making crazy patterns in the water. Her face, free now of grease-paint or powder though still a little animated, like that of a child at play, was perfectly modelled, a little full about the mouth and nose, with the sensuality, maybe, of an artist. Her eyes were green.

Gone was her finery of the night before. She wore a simple riding habit of grey, the demure frills of a white shirtwaist peeping above the collar. The skirt was long but she had hitched it up a little, revealing a shapely calf, from just below the knee to where the ankle was distorted in the shimmering water.

Her riding boots and the woollen socks that went with them were on the grass just behind her. So was her wide-brimmed bowler-type hat.

The paint pony was cropping grass back a little way in the glade.

She sensed something near her. She thought it was the pony who had come down to the water for a drink. But the little movements she had heard suddenly ceased: she had a feeling of being watched, of eyes crawling all over. Swiftly she pulled her skirt down lower.

She saw the reflection of the man in the water. It moved, then was motionless, a tall rippling figure. As she turned, her hand went inside the breast of her riding jacket.

A voice said: 'Put up your hands, lady. Don't make any more sudden movements.'

Slowly she raised her hands. She looked into the muzzle of a gun held in the steady hand of a slim man clothed all in black.

She looked up into his face. Handsome, young, dark, curiously smooth. His eyes, they made the sun turn cold and she shivered.

'You can stand up, lady,' he said.

She heard herself say through dry lips. 'I'll have to use my hands.'

'All right. Use them. Use them carefully.'

She began to rise. 'What do you want?' she said. 'What do you want?'

He did not answer. She stood before him, her naked feet on the grass. His face was impersonal, his dark eyes gave nothing away, but somehow she felt ashamed. As if she was naked all over. More even than when she was on the stage – although that had never seemed the same. That was her art, her job . . .

Her shame turned suddenly to indignation, mingled with fear, as he came towards her.

'You coward!' she said. 'Holding up a woman . . . What do you want?' Her voice faltered as he came nearer. It was as if she hadn't spoken.

He seemed to move incredibly swiftly then. He was upon her, his gun-hand went around her shoulders, his other inside her coat, to the derringer in the little shoulder holster there. When he stepped back, his own gun was back in its sheath and he was weighing the other little weapon in his hand.

She forgot her fear in her indignation at this other shame he had put upon her. Her body went hot and cold by turns. Her face was burning.

'How dare you touch me!'

'I didn't want to touch you. You had a gun.' His voice was like dripping ice. Was it her fancy or had the mahogany hue of his face deepened a little.

Studying him she suddenly realized who he was. But she was not scared of him any more.

'You're Johnny Salom,' she said.

His lips curled a little. 'You're Annabella Strudel.' His voice was flat – horrible. She said:

'What does Johnny Salom want with me?'

'I want nothing with you. I just want my paint pony.'

He might have lashed her across the face. 'What do you think you are?' she said. 'A gaol-bird. A killer . . .'

His level voice cut in on her tirade. 'You won't have to walk into town. I've brought another horse along with me.'

'That's very kind of you,' she sneered. 'Take your pony and get away from me.'

He bowed slightly, awkwardly. Her words had had no other effect on him. His face was still marble-like.

Suddenly his hand moved. 'Catch,' he said. Insinctively she threw her hand up and caught the spinning derringer. His own gun had appeared like magic in his hand. 'Put it away,' he said. 'An' don't try to draw it on me again . . .'

'You're despicable!' She put the derringer in its holster, thinking of the way his hand had taken it smoothly from there. She went suddenly cold again, watching those dark eyes beneath the wide brimmed sombrero.

He had holstered his gun and was turning when the other voice spoke.

'Elevate 'em, kid!'

He turned, then froze, his hand clawed a couple of inches above the butt of his gun. Then slowly he raised that hand; then the other one.

The lean man in scarred leather chaps came through the trees, behind him two more palpable cowhands. They all had guns in their fists.

'I'm surprised at you, Kid,' drawled the lean man. 'I didn't think you wuz the sort to molest women.'

Johnny Salom did not deign to answer. He watched the

three men with his head a little bent, his eyes in the
shadow of his hat-brim giving nothing away. His body had
the tension of a coiled spring.

'Move over aways, miss,' said the lean man.

Annabella Strudel picked up her shoes and socks
and hat and backed slowly along the bank of the creek.
She had her wide green eyes on the men all the time.
Presently she stopped and began, still standing, to put
on her socks and boots. With little jerks of her head she
still watched the men.

'Take his gun, Happy,' said the lean man. 'You, Lem,
go get his hoss.'

'All right, Slim,' Lem moved away. Happy, whose
lugubrious visage pointed the humour of his nickname,
moved forward. Gun in hand, he went around Johnny
Salom in a half-circle, and came up behind him.

The kid's gun hung low, forward a little for a quick
draw: a flick of the wrist, a shot from the hip. A swivel
attached the holster to the gun-belt. A man had to be
fast to use that kind of a gadget: if he was at all clumsy
it was liable to slide from under him, like an iced lemon
in a tumbler of liquor.

Happy was the jerky type. His wasn't the smooth,
swift draw of the born gunfighter. He grabbed the butt
of the gun and it slid from beneath his palm like a
greased stick. Taken by surprise he lurched forward a
little, grabbed again. The gun tipped from the holster
and fell to the ground.

Johnny Salom's arm flashed down. The chopping
edge of his palm hit the back of Happy's neck. Happy
gulped and sagged at the knees, trying frantically to

bring his gun up. The arm curved round his neck in a throttling grip, the kid's other hand reached out for the gun. Happy flailed with it and felt his man wince . . . Then they were grappling. While Slim danced up and down like a scalded cat, the gun in his hand, useless. Happy's back was to him. His gun was waving around as he tried to keep it away from his assailant who had hold of his sleeve.

Slim began to walk forward, catfooted, the barrel of the gun elevated a little, ready for a quick swing at the kid's head if he had a chance at it.

Suddenly Happy let out a yelp and dropped his gun. Johnny Salom pushed him aside and dived for the weapon. Slim's iron spoke, smoke curled. The gun beneath the kid's hand jumped and spun. Johnny straightened up.

'All right,' said Slim. 'We'll have no more capers like that. Unless you want to dance on the end of a rope – pronto!'

The whole action had not taken more than a few seconds and when Lem came running back to the creek everything was over. Silent, unsmiling, the unarmed Yaqui Kid stood under Slim's gun. Behind him the disgruntled Happy was picking up his own and the captive's weapon.

Lem led two horses forward. The paint pony and the bigger one.

'I dunno which is his'n,' he said.

Johnny Salom spoke then. 'That's mine,' pointing to the paint.

A shrill voice said: 'No it isn't. That's the one I came

53

on,' and Annabella Strudel, fully dressed now, came forward.

'I guess he ain't in no particular need of a hoss anyway,' said Slim. 'Maybe we oughta string him up right here an' now to save the trouble o' drivin' him back to town. I never did cotton to geezers who molest defenceless women . . .'

The girl blanched a little. 'He – he didn't do anything to me,' she said. 'I mean . . . he said he'd just come after his horse . . .'

'His hoss?'

'Yes, he said that paint pony was his horse.'

'Is it?'

The girl hesitated. Johnny Salom spoke flatly. 'I left him in town last night. They put him in the livery-stables. I came for him this mornin' an' the stableman tol' me that this young lady had borrowed him . . .'

'You came back to Tucson while this hue-an'-cry's on jest on account o' thet hoss?' said Slim.

'I felt lost without him,' said the Yaqui Kid. It was an unsentimental statement of fact.

'Jumpin' Jesophat,' said Slim. 'Pardner you take the biscuit.'

'He can have the horse,' said Annabella Strudel in a very small voice.

The Yaqui Kid bowed slightly. 'Thank you, lady,' he said flatly.

She did not look at him. She faced Slim but her eyes were downcast as she said:

'You're not goin' to do . . . what you said?'

'Nope,' said Slim. 'We Texans don't do things like

54

that. We like to give a man an even break. A man kind of gets attached to a particular hoss. I've got one like that myself right now – had him since he wuz knee-high to a grasshopper, wouldn't part wi' him f'r a bag o' gold. I can understand this young fellah's feelings. I didn't give him credit for such sentiments I guess. Not that I don't think he's plumb crazy . . .'

'Hey, Slim!' put in Lem suddenly, 'there's hosses comin'.'

Slim stopped talking. The little group became motionless. Faintly to them came the drum of horses' hoofs. Slim said: 'Git on that pony, Salom . . . All of yuh get mounted.'

The kid got on the paint and Annabella on the larger horse. She mounted rather awkwardly and still she did not look at him.

'Watch him, Lem,' said Slim. 'Happy, you come with me.'

He kneed his horse forward through the cotton-woods. Happy shot a mournful look back at the others and followed.

'Sit tight,' said Lem. 'An' keep yore hands where I kin see 'em.'

Johnny Salom put his hands on the saddle pommel and sat looking straight in front of him. Annabella sat her horse and felt acutely uncomfortable. From under lowered lids she threw a covert glance at the dark young man sitting like a graven statue. There was no hint of strain or fear in his bearing. Annabella shuddered to think of that lean, perfectly-modelled body swinging at the end off a rope. An Easterner, unused to these wilder ways, she found it hard to understand their rough justice, administered sometimes on the spot, as Slim had hinted. Her blood ran cold at the thought of it.

She had despised Johnny Salom. A killer she had called him. By her Eastern standards he was that and more. But his courage was undeniable. To rise in her profession she had fought herself against seemingly overwhelming odds . . . Well, touring the West with a dancing troupe was not the apex of her ambition but at least it was a measure of success, and freedom from poorly-paid chorus work in the big cities, the attentions of men . . . What kind of attentions had Johnny Salom paid her? He had touched her. But only to take her gun. All he had wanted was his horse! Suddenly she felt like laughing aloud.

She wondered if anything could ever move that Indianlike creature. Maybe if they took him and hanged him by the neck . . . She shuddered again, almost throwing her hands up over her eyes to shut out the horrible sight, which her mind had projected for her. She realized that she had had a complete reversal of feelings. She wanted Johnny Salom to get away. To have another chance. No matter what he was, what he had done, it seemed important to her that he should have another chance.

Slim and Happy returned through the trees. The former said:

'It's thet pesky bartender an' his boss, Craig Jepson. An' two, three other officious-lookin' galoots.' He shook his head from side to side. 'I tol' thet fat liquor-washer to git from under my feet. I'll have to take him apart an' see what makes him tick. An' thet Jepson – him an' his sort get in my craw.' He looked from one to the other of his pardners. 'What say we do?'

'You're the boss,' said Happy sullenly.

'I ain't aiming to see nobody railroaded,' said Lem. Slim looked at Annabella. 'What do you say, miss?' he said softly. 'Craig Jepson's a friend o' yourn, ain't be? Shall we hand the Yaqui Kid here over to him all tied up with a ribbon?'

The girl flushed and bit her lip. 'Mr Jepson's no friend of mine,' she said, with emphasis on the 'friend.' 'He just gave my troupe and me an engagement that's all. I should imagine him to be a very vindictive man and, unlike Texans, not so likely to give anybody an even break.'

Slim bowed. 'Nicely spoken, Miss Annabella,' he said.

The girl dropped her eyes. She felt that Johnny Salom was looking at her, too. The glimpse that she had told her that there was something like puzzlement in his eyes.

'Give the kid his gun, Happy,' said Slim. 'Quick about it.'

Happy, his face longer than ever, kneed his horse forward and handed Johnny Salom his Colt, butt foremost. The latter took it and dropped it into his holster and, as Happy moved aside, still sat his motionless horse.

Slim said: 'Get goin', yuh crazy galoot, an' I hope you give 'em a run f'r their money. An' if you come into Tucson again on the rampage remember to only shoot at folks you know. There's plenty o' my boys knockin' around.'

The two men exchanged glances. Something unspoken passed between them: they understood each other. Their guards were down for a split-second in which each man paid his silent tribute to the other.

Johnny Salom did not say 'thank you' or 'so long.' He did not say anything. He just turned his horse around and kneed it forward.

As he passed Annabella their eyes met for a moment. Then he was past and gone and she did not know whether it was her imagination or not that those bleak dark orbs had softened a little as he gave his almost imperceptible bow. Then the paint pony had straightened out like an arrow flashing from a bow and its rider was flat over its neck. They were blended in speed, streaking into the heat-haze, out to the horizon.

Craig Jepson rode through the cottonwoods and shouted. Four horsemen went past him, among them the paunchy barman; they galloped in the wake of the Yaqui Kid.

Jepson drew his horse to a stop before Slim.

'Why didn't you do something?' he said. 'Why didn't you stop him? Why didn't you shoot at him?' Slim spat in the dust directly alongside the right front hoof of the other's horse. He eyed the drying spittle with interest. Then he said:

'Do your own chasing, mister.'

He kneed his horse forward, passing Jepson without another look. His pardners followed his trail.

Annabella Strudel said: 'I'll ride back to town with you.'

'You're welcome, miss,' said Slim.

She said 'Good morning' to Jepson as she passed him.

His eyes were fixed on Slim's long straight back. There was a very nasty look in his eyes. His answer was purely mechanical.

As she was catching up with the three Texans Annabella looked back. As she did so Jepson turned his horse and set off in the wake of his men.

She looked that way. There was no sign of Johnny Salom or his pursuers – only the sombre black-coated figure of the horseman going along the creek in the direction they had taken.

SIX

Great was the rage of Marshal Cuthbertson and his minions when they learnt that, whilst they had been rampaging across the countryside, their quarry had calmly returned to Tucson and created another furore there. That he had tied up Jose, the livery-stable keeper after first frightening him half to death, that he had recovered his pony, alleged to be the only reason why he had returned: that he had had conversation with Annabella Strudel, the dancer and, it seemed with the straw-boss of the Texan cowboys and two of his pards – who had him, and then didn't have him . . .

Tongues were clacking. People said that the marshal had, since he came back, questioned Miss Strudel and had been bulldozed at every point, and that Craig Jepson had insisted that the three Texans be arrested for helping the Yaqui Kid to escape. The three rannies in question appeared large as life in the Golden Wheel that same night. Men looked at them askance. They were inclined to be mighty sore at these happy-go-lucky strangers who, because they had brought some prime beef into the Tucson pens, seemed to think they could do as they damwell pleased.

But there were more of them than just three. A damsight more. They were everywhere. Swaggering in their chaps and high-heeled boots. Their soft drawl all around like a hive of bees. They had finished their job, they had been paid, they had a few weeks to kill before returning home. They were high-spirited, and out for a good time, like children if humoured, but quick to anger. Catering for them was like feeding a wild colt and, after this mornin's furore, in which the boss of the trail-drive, one Slim, and his two pards had largely figured, the hospitality of Tucson was becoming a little strained . . . these strangers did not seem to realize that the Yaqui Kid was a thorn in the side of the fair township . . .

That night, the three Texans, greeted on all sides by their pardners, strode up to the bar as if nothing had happened. The paunchy barman was the nearest hand: Slim called him. The man approached a little diffi-dently.

'Three doubles,' said Slim, his face and voice totally expressionless.

The other man's pudgy visage wore an uncertain look as he turned to the liquor shelves. He poured the drinks and turned again. Slim gave him a bill. He took it away, returned with the change. Slim said conversa-tionally:

'So yuh didn't catch the Yaqui Kid?'

'No,' said the barman.

Slim leaned closer across the bar, his elbow came up and across in a sweeping motion, skittling the three glasses of whiskey. The liquor splashed over the front of

61

the barman's vest, above his white apron. The glasses smashed to smithereens at the man's feet. He started back, mopping at himself with podgy hands, his face going a queer mottled colour.

'Somebody's always gettin' under my feet,' expostulated Slim. He threw another bill on top of the bar. 'Make three more, pardner – pronto!'

The barman whitened a little, looking about him like a harried beast. But nobody seemed to have noticed the incident except an old-timer who was grinning all over his bearded face.

The fat man filled three more glasses and placed them gingerly on the bar. Slim reached for the glass furthest away from him. Like a hypnotized rabbit the barman watched the reaching fingers. The inevitability of it all seemed to hold him rooted to the spot. His face was mottled over again and there was a queer glazed light in his eyes.

Slim's pards gazed around the saloon. Slim's hand scrabbled at the glass, grabbed it awkwardly. Then it seemed to slip. The barman started back as whiskey gushed once more, the potent smell of it rising into his nostrils.

His eyes bulged from his head. His mouth yammered. Then the words came out in a rush as he dived sideways, his hands reaching under the bar.

'You're not gonna haze me! I'll show yuh. I'll . . .' The muzzle of a shotgun came up above the bar.

Slim's right hand had disappeared: it came into view again, sweeping in an arc, steel gleaming. The barrel of the shotgun hit the bar with a ringing sound, the fat man staggered backwards, his hands flying up to his, face, the fingers spreading, clawing, as blood gushed through them.

'I told yuh not to get under my feet, pardner,' said Slim softly.

It was doubtful if the barman heard him this time. Moaning, his head down, blood dripping through his fingers he blundered and groped. His partner, yelling ran from the other end of the bar. He pulled up short at the gun in Slim's hand, the menace of the narrowed eyes in the lean immobile face.

The fat barman flopped and sat down on an upturned box. He rocked gently from side to side with his head in his hands. He made little hissing sounds of pain while the blood formed a small red pool between his feet.

By now nearly everybody in the room had become aware of the disturbance. There were some ugly murmurs. Slim leaned his hip against the bar, his gun sloping in his hand. He seemed to be looking both ways at once. His pardners had their backs to the bar. They had their guns out now. They weren't watching anybody in particular. The townsfolk of Tucson surged together and muttered. The walls on all sides seemed to be propped up by cowhands with thumbs in their belts – strangers from across the Texan border.

Slim said: 'Somebody better fix this fellah. He's bleedin' all over the place. But he shouldn't pull a blunderbuss on peaceful folk an' he wouldn't get hurt. . .'

'Peaceful he said . . .' began somebody.

A louder voice broke in. 'Get a doc for Pongo.'

'Here he is,' said somebody else.

A lean man with a face like an intelligent horse forced his way through the crowd. He ignored the three men with guns and climbed over the bar.

He made Pongo lift his head.

The barman's cheek had been laid open by the sharp barrel of the gun. The doctor induced him to rise and they made for the stairs. As they began to climb Craig Jepson descended towards them. They met him half way.

The saloon-owner could be seen gestulating and mouthing, his lean face pale in the light. The doctor kept nodding, while Pongo stood, a beaten hulk. Then the two men passed on and Jepson came down into the bar-room. The crowd parted to let him through. He strode forward and confronted the nonchalant Slim who had a cigarette in his chops.

Even when Jepson stopped walking he could not keep still. He was trembling with suppressed rage. His voice was strained, the words halting when they finally came out.

'What do you mean . . . What do you mean by it?' His bandaged hand pawed the air in front of him.

Slim drawled: 'The gink got nasty 'cos I spilled some liquor on him. He pulled a blunderbuss from under the bar. I hadda slug him; he might've killed two – three people. He might've even hit me the way he wuz pointin' the thing . . .'

The old-timer along the bar spoke up, his whiskers waggling as he grinned.

'Mighty dangerous fellah that Pongo. A real ring-tailed littul bobcat. Might've been hell tuh pay if this young fellah hadn't acted like he did . . .'

Jepson ignored him. 'I'll have you run outa town,' he said. 'The whole damn bunch of you . . .'

'You don't own Tucson, mister,' said Slim.

The tension in the rest of the room grew apace as the altercation went on. Jepson was working himself into a fury but he seemed loth to back his mouth with a play. He was not a popular man but for once the Tucson people were on his side. Other pockets of dispute broke out in different parts of the huge room.

Suddenly a thick voice yelled, 'String 'em up. String the damn grasshoppers higher'n . . .' There was the sound of a scuffle and the voice ended in a gurgle, the sharp smack-smack of blows.

Two Tucson men turned on the cowboy who had felled the loud-mouthed one. He went down but two more Texans stepped into his place. The small whirlpool of action began to widen. Then it seemed to explode with a great gush and the whole saloon went mad.

2

Chairs and tables went over with a crash as fighting men flung themselves across them. Slim and his two pards exchanged grins and holstered their guns. The old-timer's grin widened until it threatened to split his hairy visage. He spat on his horny hands and vanished forthwith into the mêlée.

Craig Jepson turned and a look of unutterable anguish came into his face as he saw his place being wrecked before his eyes. He threw up his hands and yelled. Nobody took any notice of him.

He whirled as Slim came nearer. 'You buzzard!' he snarled and went for his gun with his good left hand.

Slim made a huge stride and lashed out. Jepson caught the blow on the side of the jaw. His hand flew away from his gun as he staggered sideways.

A big man hurtled out of the mêlée and, head down, crashed into the lean Texan. Slim went down with the man on top of him. He flailed out with both fists at this totally unexpected assailant. The man was a dead weight upon him. Rolling him off Slim realized he was already unconscious, bleeding from a nasty gash behind his ear. He had been unconscious when he hurtled across the room.

Slim rose. Jepson was rising too and he had his gun out. There was naked murder in his eyes. Slim's usually lethargic pardner seemed to spring from nowhere. His foot shot out and Jepson yelped as it connected with his shoulder. His gun skittled away across the floor, amid trampling feet. The cowboy came nearer and the sole of his boot clamped down on Jepson's neck driving it into the boards. He held it there while Slim advanced. The two men solemnly shook hands. Then they both turned abruptly, left the squirming saloon-owner and dived into the milling crowd.

Somebody threw a bottle, which crashed into a shelf, bringing it down and a varied supply of bottled liquor with it. Glass crashed again at the other side of the room as a chair was flung through a window. The batwings flapped like shutters in a breeze as men pitched through them. Two men, locked together and clawing and spitting like wild cats, rolled beneath them, rose to their feet on the boardwalk and, toe to toe, slugged each other. Finally one of them landed a terrific blow that sent his opponent crashing against the hitching rail, splitting it in twain, and depositing him on his back in the dust.

The victor dusted off his hands and retraced his rather uneven steps through the batwings. Inside he was met by one of his vanquished opponent's pards who slammed him flush in the teeth and sent him flying outside again. His boot-heels screamed on the boardwalk. He teetered, then went over backwards. He finished up on his back beside his erstwhile foe.

The batwings swung wider and wider, as if animated by a rising wind. The scene inside the saloon was revealed like a crazy kaleidoscope. A man slid on his back along the top of the bar, skittling bottles and glasses in the process. He rolled off finally and finished up seated against a barrel with a silly look on his face.

Many men joined him in the long well behind the bar. Some of them lay still. Others stirred feebly and groped, grasped a convenient bottle, uncorked it and took a swig. Invariably, after that, they decided to stay where they were in comfort and comparative safety – until another hurtling body descended on them, seemingly from the clouds.

A flying bottle smashed one of the hanging lights, making that end of the room a place of shadows. Men pranced and wrestled there like strange creatures, throwing fantastic shapes on the walls and ceiling.

Two slugging rannies carried the fight up onto the stage. Finally they got tangled up in the curtain, bringing it down on the heads of those immediately below. Men squirmed and fought beneath it or crawled from under to meet fresh attacks.

The two cowboys waltzed round the stage like a couple of professionals. Finally, with a mighty swing one of them sent his opponent tumbling from it to join the curtain, which was animated by fluctuating bumps and hillocks.

The victor had the stage to himself. He was a big gent with flaming red hair and he strutted like the king of the castle, daring anybody to come and fetch him down. A smaller man darted up the steps, brandishing a chair leg. The red-head met him with a contemptuous swing – so contemptuous that it missed. The little fellow darted under the bear-like arms and swung the chair-leg. The big man yelled and jumped as it cracked across his knees. It swung again, higher up this time, and the red-head doubled up. A smack on the back of his red-thatched pate finished him off. His bulk sprawled across the stage, an unconscious Goliath.

The little fellow leapt nimbly down. The curtain was flattening out as men extricated themselves from it and crawled from under. The little man pranced around, hitting heads sharply with his chair leg. He was doing fine until a huge miner picked him up by the scruff of his neck and the seat of his pants and tossed him through the nearest window, which, luckily, hadn't any glass left in it.

The tide of battle moved away from the little musicians dais so the players, as yet unscathed, took up their places once more. In the hopes of creating a diversion they struck up a catchy tune.

68

The trouble started when the banjo player had his instrument snatched from his hand and turned into a ruff for his neck. That gave people ideas. The pianist's head was thrust through the front of his jingle-box which, fortunately for him, was only made of mesh. Kicking wildly to extricate himself he sent the instrument crashing from the dais with a harsh jangle of keys.

The fiddle-player and the drummer were not so easily vanquished. The former used his instrument like a flail, clearing a place for himself. The kettle-drum was held like a shield by its owner, who armed himself with his stool and leapt from his perch to do battle.

A bruised and battered Craig Jepson crawled from under trampling feet, rose and made a dash for the batwings. He was yelling like mad for the marshal when he cannoned into that worthy. Cuthbertson had a few staunch members of the community with him. They breasted the batwings and the big man bawled 'Stop it!' at the pitch of his lungs. Nobody took any notice. A bottle sailed from the other end of the room and knocked the marshal's hat off. Craig Jepson cried out in anguish as the beautiful figured mirror behind the bar was shattered to smithereens by a chair. Then he began to yell and wave his arms about.

Lafe Cuthbertson bent slowly and deliberately and picked up his hat. He clapped it back on his head. Then he drew his gun and fired four rapid shots into the ceiling. Jepson moaned again as plaster fell in showers.

When the echoes of the shots died away there was comparative silence as men stopped fighting and looked around them. When guns were let off that was the time to call a halt before folks got slaughtered.

'Who started this?' bawled the marshal.

'It was that lanky straw-boss,' shrilled Craig Jepson. Slim bobbed up out of the crowd. He had a black eye and a triangular gash in his cheek. His right shirt-sleeve had been torn away, revealing his lean muscular arm.

He said: 'You're talkin' through the back of your neck, mister. You know damwell yar fat barman, Pongo, pulled a blunderbuss on me. You're lucky nobody ain't kilt outright . . .'

'You're nothing but trouble-makers, the whole damn' lot of you,' said Jepson.

Others took up his cry and were answered by the Texan herders in no uncertain tones.

'Easy,' bawled the marshal. 'Quiet everybody. Let's get this figured out before there's any more bloodshed.'

His broad moustached face did not reveal his feelings, This was a time when lots of diplomacy was called for. If anybody went haywire and pulled a gun the balloon would go up with a vengeance.

The din died to sullen murmurs. The marshal was opening his mouth to speak again when there was a loud cry from outside. Then a man came running through the batwings yelling:

'He's here again! The Yaqui Kid's here again! The Yaqui Kid!'

Everybody seemed transfixed for a moment. Then there was a stampede for the door, sweeping the marshal with it.

SEVEN

Flames gushed suddenly at the end of the street. A man came running towards the mob yelling:

'The cantina. The cantina's on fire!'

Stumbling from the saloon in the wake of the rest Craig Jepson groaned aloud. The cantina belonged to him. He began to run.

There were already a sizeable amount of folks outside the place, passing buckets of water from hand to hand to throw on the flames. The name of the Yaqui Kid was on every lip.

'Where is he?' bawled the marshal. 'Where's he gone?'

A bunch of men accosted the lawman. They had been chasing the Kid on foot and had lost him along the 'backs' someplace.

'Is he still in town?'

They weren't sure. One said: 'I figure he must've had his hoss stashed someplace. He's probably miles away. We couldn't hear anythin' 'cos o' the ruckus from the saloon . . .'

Craig Jepson, blundering forward, heard the last few words. He grabbed hold of the marshal's sleeve.

'Don't you see,' he said. 'It was a put-up job. Those Texan's started a fight in the saloon to draw attention away from here while the Kid did his work. They're in league with him. . . .'

'That needs thinking about.'

'A-ah!' said Jepson. He staggered forward a little, yelling 'Jose. Where's Jose?'

'Here he is,' said somebody else. A little fat Mexican stumbled forward into the glare of the flames.

His black eyes were shining, his hair hung over his forehead in damp ringlets, his face was streaming with sweat.

Jepson bounded forward and caught hold of him by the shoulders. He began to shake him like a madman, shouting:

'Where've you been? What happened? What did he do? . . .' and other sentences which were little more than obscene gibberish.

The marshal's huge hand grabbed his shoulder and pulled him away from the quaking man. Jepson quietened down.

'Pull yourself together, Jose,' said Cuthbertson. 'Nobody's gonna hurt yuh. Tell us what happened.'

The stuttering Mexican, who was proprietor and cook for Jepson's cantina, began to tell his garbled story.

He had been working in his kitchen when the Yaqui Kid came in the back way and held him up with a gun. He drove him outside, shoved him into the barn and locked him in, telling him that if he kicked up a ruckus he'd come back and shoot him in the belly.

He kept quiet. All he heard after that was somebody shouting 'Fire! Fire!' When he tried the door he found it was unlocked. The Kid must have slipped back and unlocked it. Jose crept out to discover the back of the cantina in flames before him and nobody around at all.

A man detached himself from the group that had surrounded Cuthbertson, Jepson and the Mexican. This worthy took up the tale, backed up now and then by folks behind him.

He, together with about five others – everybody else had run down to the Golden Wheel – had been sitting at tables eating when the Yaqui Kid appeared at the counter with a gun in each hand.

He calmly told them that the place was on fire and that they'd better get out pronto unless they wanted to get roasted. Then he vanished into the back.

When they had gotten over their surprise they followed. They were beaten back by flames. There was no sign of the Kid.

They returned, ran out into the street and gave the alarm.

'What did he take?' said Jepson. 'What did he take?'

'I didn't see him take nuthin'!'

'We'll never know whether he took anything or not now,' said the marshal drily as the cantina collapsed with a *whoosh* and a crash and a shower of sparks.

Craig Jepson looked like he would burst into tears.

'That young jasper has certainly got it in for you,' said the marshal.

The saloon-owner turned on him furiously. 'Those Texans were part of it. I demand you arrest them—'

'Git off your high hoss, Mr Jepson,' said Cuthbertson.

Jepson opened his mouth to say something else. He left it open, yammering soundlessly as a voice yelled:

'The bank's bin robbed! Where's the marshal? Somebody's busted into the bank—'

'Here I am,' boomed Cuthbertson. Then his voice was drowned by other cries as the whole crowd, fire-fighters and all, turned about and washed in a noisy tide towards the bank.

Craig Jepson cast one look back at the slowly burning remains of his cantina and followed the lawman. The man who had yelled in the first place jogged to the marshal's side. In breathless pants he said:

'I heerd a scufflin' sound in there an' muffled cries like somebody was tryin' to shout. I pushed the door and it opened. I found Jasper Lynecote tied to a chair an' gagged in his office. I cut him loose an' run out for you right away . . .'

Just then somebody shouted: 'Here's Jasper,' and the portly banker tottered towards the crowd.

Cuthbertson charged forward and caught Lynecote's arm.

Followed by the mob he led him, spluttering inco-herently, back into the darkness of the bank. Inch Lemmings slipped in behind them and Craig Jepson and one or two more.

'Lock the doors,' said Cuthbertson. 'We don't want the whole damn' town in here.'

74

It was the blocky Inch who got his shoulder against the door and pushed it into the faces of the advancing crowd. An arm came around its edge and Inch hit it hard with his fist. A man yowled and the arm was withdrawn. Inch slammed the door and locked it. Inside the bank now, besides himself, were the marshal; the banker and the man who had found him; Craig Jepson; Jeb Downs, the little printer and his lanky assistant, Cracker. These latter two seemed to have materialized from nowhere. Jeb already had his notebook out and his pencil poised.

Portly Jasper Lynecote had regained his composure. 'Step into my office, gentlemen,' he said with a return of his old pomposity.

They trooped after him into the lamplit room. He flopped down in his swivel chair and mopped his face with a large white handkerchief.

The marshal, his face grim, stood straddle-legged the other side of the desk. The others fanned out into different positions around the room.

'Don' keep us waitin', Jasper,' said the marshal.

Lynecote blew out his cheeks and glared indignantly. 'I've had a terrible experience . . .'

'All right, tell us about it.'

'Er-rumph,' said Jasper. 'Yes . . . Well, I was retiring. Er – as you know, gentleman, I live alone. My housekeeper had long since gone. I was mounting the stairs when I heard a knock on the back door . . . I've always believed in taking elementary precautions, so I got my gun before I went out there. When I opened the door there was nobody there. I stepped outside a little – I realize now, gentlemen, that that was a very foolish thing to do – it was just what my visitor was waiting for. He came out of the side and stuck a gun in my ribs. He took my own gun out of my hand then pushed me back into the kitchen.

'He was a young man, lean, well-built. A queer-looking fellah. Dark, handsome but with a smooth expressionless face and queer dark eyes. They gave me the creeps. His voice matched them. It was stony . . .'

Simultaneous murmurs of 'Johnny Salom' and 'The Kid' came from the assembled company.

'He was dressed all in black,' said Lynecote.

'It was the Kid all right,' said Cuthbertson. 'Go on, Jasper.'

'He asked me if I had my keys to the bank. I could see there was no use shilly-shallying, he looked quite capable of killing me and taking them from my body, so I produced them. He told me to get up, that we were going for a little walk. Then he took me outside and drove me all along the backs of the houses to the bank. He made me open up then, when we got inside he said all he wanted was Craig Jepson's deposit box . . .'

'My box!' It was a cry of anguish from the dishevelled saloon-owner. 'What did you do?'

'What do you think I did,' said Lynecote with a sudden spurt of dry humour. 'I've got more sense than to argue with a loaded gun. I gave it to him.'

'Funny, isn't it?' snarled Jepson, his teeth bared.

The marshal cut in. 'He didn't take anything else?'

'Not a thing,' said the banker. 'He tied me to this chair and gagged me. Then he went.'

'How long ago was this?'

'About twenty minutes. I was here quite a bit before this gentleman found me.' The banker nodded at his deliverer.

'So while we were prancing around blowin' at the fire the Kid was making good his getaway . . .'

Craig Jepson leapt to his feet. 'Can't you see?' he shrilled. 'It was all planned. The fight in the saloon, the fire – all directed at me. Those Texans were in it too . . .'

'It certainly looks that way,' said Cuthbertson. 'But why the Texans? And why should everything be directed at you? Can you answer that?'

Sinking back into his seat, his passion dying again, Jepson shook his head dumbly.

Jack Lemmings said: 'Mebbe it's because he's the richest man in town.'

Inch was a blocky, taciturn good-natured hombre who worked with old Jake Cornfield, the blacksmith. He had no particular pardner and was wont to roam all over the place on his lonesome when he wasn't working. So when he rode out of Tucson the morning after that memorably hectic night nobody took an atom of notice.

Once out of sight of the town he goaded his mount's lope into a steady gallop. He rode like a man with a purpose and in a great hurry.

Presently he veered off the trail, leaving the richer grasslands behind and beginning to cross a plain of scrubbier stuff, stuff, broken by patches of sand and mesquite and outcrops of rock. To the left of him, fluctuating in the heat-haze, the blue caps of the hills began to show.

He passed through a cluster of huge fantastic-shaped boulders and the ground fell away suddenly beneath his horse's feet. He reined-in on the slope and looked down into the valley. About two miles away lay the cluster of tepees which was the new Yaqui village. The blocky redhaired man sat motionlessly erect in the saddle for a few moments, then kneed his horse down the slope.

The gradient was less steep, and the tepees were becoming so clear to his sight that he could count them, when he saw two horsemen break away from there and come galloping towards him.

As they drew nearer he saw they were Indians, naked to the waist and with feathers in their long hair. They came nearer. They wore fringed buckskin trousers and their feet were bare. They rode without stirrups and their only saddles were a strip of blanket flung across the horses' backs.

They rode their small cayuses without a bit or bridle but with a halter around their noses and strips of reins attached. They came on more slowly and finally halted a few yards from Inch. He raised his hand in salute and spoke a few bastardized words of their language. He continued to ride forward.

They regarded him impassively, sitting their horses like lean bronze statues. He was almost upon them when they split apart, turned their horses, and rode alongside him towards the village.

Inch's square red face wore an expression of almost

ludicrous gravity as he passed in among the tepees. He was very conscious of the honour they had bestowed on him in allowing him, a white man, to enter so easily into their home. That they did it not for his worth alone but because he was a friend of one of their 'blood-brothers' did not alter the situation one jot. Curious glances were thrown at him by squaws and bright-eyed children.

They led him, without a word, to the centre of the camp. Here in a cleared space stood a tepee, as drab as its fellows, but distinguished from them by the fact that it was larger and that its centre pole had a fragment of coloured ribbon flying from it. Before its door was an upturned packing case laid with skins.

One of the Yaqui's dismounted and, after motioning to his companions and the white man to stay where they were, stooped and entered the tepee.

Seconds passed and then he returned. He took up a position at the stirrup of Inch's horse and stood immobile, his arms folded. A very old Indian came out of the tent and raised his hand in greeting. He hobbled to the improvised throne and sank down upon it. Inch dismounted from his horse, strode forward a few paces and went down on one knee in front of the wizened, brown man, as if in deference to his age. The old man extended a shrivelled paw and they shook hands white man fashion.

Inch spoke haltingly in the old man's language, using his hands when he was at a loss for a word. The ancient chief's eyes were as bright as a bird's in the incredibly wrinkled face. He spoke with little nods and shakes of his head.

Presently he looked past Inch and spoke a few rapid words to his two men. Both of them turned away, taking their own horses and Inch's with them. A few seconds later one of them returned and placed a buffalo robe before the white man. Inch nodded his thanks and squatted cross-legged upon it.

He took the makings from his pocket and rolled a quirly. The old man's little sloe-eyes brightened as they watched him. The way he did it, with two fingers of one hand, intrigued the Indian mind. Inch finished the cigarette and handed it to the chief, who took it, examining it carefully as if reluctant to put it to his mouth.

Inch produced a shiny-backed book of lucifers, tore one off, and struck it on his thumb-nail. He lit the cigarette for the old man who coughed a bit at first, then settled down to a steady puffing that ate the weed away at a surprising rate.

Inch rolled another one, stuck it into the corner of his own mouth and lit it. Seeing the chief's eyes fixed on the brightly-coloured book of lucifers he handed it over with a little bow.

Already the old man had finished the cigarette, not throwing the glowing stub away until it was in danger of scorching his lips.

Anticipating his want, Inch rolled him another one. The old man's eyes gleamed like a michievous young buck's as he tore a lucifer of and lit the cigarette with it.

At this juncture an Indian youth ran into the clearing and called out something shrilly. The chief held his hand out to Inch who gave him his arm and helped him to rise. Inch turned about and they faced the man who approached them. It was Johnny Salom.

He saluted the old chief with an uplifted palm and a slight bow that had in it a hint of gentle courtesy. He then caught hold of Inch's outstretched hand and shook it. His dark face was as impassive as any Indian's but there seemed to be a warmer light in his eyes.

He spoke a few words in fluent dialect to the chief and gave him his arm too. The two men led the old man back into his tepee then, side by side, they walked to the outskirts of the village. They talked in short sentences with pauses in between, as was the nature of both of them.

'You suttinly stood Tucson on it's head last night,' said Inch Lemmings.

'That unexpected shindig in the Golden Wheel was a big help,' said Johnny Salom.

'Yeh, I know, 'an' that's mainly what I wanted to see you about,' slid the red-head. 'The marshal's clapped Slim, the Texan straw-boss, an' his two pards, in the hoose-gow on account of it. Nearly everybody thinks they're in league with you an' started thet ruckus purposely in order to make it easier for you to fire the cantina an' rob the bank . . .'

'But I fired the cantina in order to draw everybody's attention while I did the bank job . . .'

'Yeh, that's what I figured. But it looks bad for that Slim. It seems he stopped Pongo, the barman, from taking a pot-shot at you yestiddy mawnin' when you were comin' from the stables. Then later, down by the crick, he let you get away. On top o' that he pistol-whipped Pongo last night and, indirectly, started thet free-for-all while you were up to your tricks in another part o' town. You gotta admit it looks mighty suspicious.'

'Yeh,' said the Kid broodingly.

'Inch went on: 'O' course, Craig Jepson's the prime mover behind it all. Every Texas cowboy in Tucson 'ud be stuck up agin a wall an' shot if he had his way. This time the marshal's listened to him – but he's got good reason to I guess . . . The rest o' the trail-herd boys don't take kindly to their boss and his *amigos* bein' clapped in gaol – they're simmering gently at the moment, but I guess that if somep'n ain't done soon all hell'll break loose. There're some mighty mean-looking gun-toters among that bunch; maybe the streets o' Tucson'll run with blood sooner than you bargained for. That'd suit your book I know. But it ain't gonna help Slim an' his pards in the long run, is it? They'll finish up either dangling on the end o' lynch-ropes or riding out on the owl-hoot— through no actual fault o' their own either . . .'

'Yeh,' said the Kid again. He paused while Inch looked into his immobile face. Then he said abruptly and with a little quirk of his lips, half between a smile and a sneer:

'Any sympathizers in town?'

Inch smiled mirthlessly too: 'I see what you mean. Wal, I guess you can count Jeb Downs, you remember how he fought for you through his paper during the trial, in the face of most o' Tucson too. An' o' course, his assistant, Cracker; he's growin' up, an' then some – I guess he'd be a handy lad in a pinch. Then o' course there's ol' Jake – an' the Salter brothers, kind of cousins o' yourn ain't they. . . ?'

'They'll fight for the side who pays 'em the most,' said Johnny Salom. His lips quirked again. 'Still, I guess I kin do that if I like now I've got most of Craig Jepson's money. It ain't no good to me for nothin' else . . . Can I fix you up with somethin', Inch . . .'

'Forget it for a bit,' said the other with an abrupt shake of his head.

Johnny Salom's next words matched his mood.

'Gimme one or two days,' he said with finality.

Inch Lemmings shrugged and said: 'All right.'

EIGHT

Annabella Strudel's adventure beside the creek did not prevent her from going there again. Rather did it lend piquancy to the morning pilgrimage: she found herself looking around her more than usual and often straining her eyes to reach the horizon. What or who she expected to see she would not admit to herself, but, always when she was by that sun-dappled water she had the feeling of something unfinished, something poised and waiting within her, a feeling of adventure which she had expected to experience in the so-called Wild West and had never done so until this time.

She ceased to sit and paddle her feet in the water but began to explore parts of the creek she had never seen before. It was during one of these explorations, when she had travelled probably further than she had ever done before, that she found the tumbledown cabin standing alone there among the tall grass and the reeds.

One glance assured her that the place must be empty: the glass-less windows, the sagging roof, the door open leaning on broken hinges. Nevertheless, to her awakened imagination there was something sinister about it, and she dismounted from her horse and advanced rather timorously. She had to wade through knee-high grass. She kicked something soft in the depths, and, bending, picked up a woman's hat: a straw hat that had once been blue but was now mildewed to a mottled colour, a draggled moth-eaten veil hanging from it.

Annabella had a sudden feeling of sadness as, holding this finery from the dim past between her thumb and forefinger, she looked around her. The gloomy feeling was suddenly replaced by one of creeping alarm; she had the feeling that someone was watching her. She looked back. The edge of town was not far away. But it was a part of Tucson she had never seen before, a hodge-podge of sagging log cabins and tumbledown shacks. Here she realized was where the outcasts lived. The wild bunch she had heard about, the Kellys, the Simkinses, the Salter brothers who seldom wore shoes and were reported to be the slickest horse-thieves in the whole state. And the women, too, who the cowhands visited when they were drunk and needy of that kind of comfort. Annabella's life had not been a bed of roses but, thinking of those women she felt that sadness creeping over her once more. She had the humility to murmur: 'There, but for the Grace of God, go I.'

Here she realized was the Tucson that had cradled Johnny Salom, even more of an outcast maybe than the Kellys and the Simkinses and the Salter brothers. Her sadness grew, and a modicum of pity too – turning to a perverse womanlike admiration for the fearless, implacable lone wolf that had been bred by this environment. She looked back at the disused, isolated cabin and fragments of a story flitted through her mind. There was no fear in her mind, only that sadness, and a curiosity, as she strode forward once more.

She pushed the sagging door a little wider and stepped into the dim interior. Then she gasped, her mouth flying open.

A voice said: 'Quiet, Miss Strudel,' and she killed the scream in her throat, cramming her fist between her teeth.

She had recognized the voice. Now she saw the man advancing out of the shadows, mincing on high-heeled riding-boots, something lean and wolfish about him. Finding him here after she had recently been thinking of him, gave her a shock that left her trembling with conflicting emotions. He halted a few yards away and was silent, as if waiting for her to speak. Finally she found her voice and said:

'What are you doing here?'

'It's my home,' he said softly. 'Leastaways, it used to be.' There was no trace of any sort of emotion in his voice which, to the girl, perversely, made the bald sentence seem even more poignant.

'You shouldn't be here,' she said. 'They'll catch you.'

'This is the last place they'll think of looking,' he said. 'Unless somebody tells 'em.'

There was nothing implied in the tone of his voice, but the girl, suddenly abnormally sensitive, chose to think there was. Her words fell swiftly yet they seemed to catch in her throat as if she tried to choke them back even as they were spoken.

'I wouldn't tell them.'

'Mebbe you wouldn't,' he said, and she was grateful for the soft gloom as she felt her face flushing. He was in shadow too, but a bright bar of sunlight fell between them as if to keep them apart. It seemed to the girl that if she crossed the narrow stream she would be committing herself to something which would be irrevocable. She began to talk again, quickly, as if to prevent herself from taking those steps that she was almost irresistibly impelled to do.

'What are you doing here? You're not living here, so close to town, are you? That's madness. You can't . . .'

His drawl cut in on her prattle. 'No. I'm not living here. I never wish to live here any more. This is the first time I've been in the place since I left it twelve years ago. I've been here since dawn, watching and waiting . . .'

'For what?'

He gave an almost imperceptible shrug: 'It's hard to say.'

'Did you see me coming?'

'Yes, I saw you.'

They were both silent again. They seemed to have reached a deadlock. The yellow stream between them was widening gradually.

He said: 'There's an old chair over here. It's rickety, but I've dusted it. Why don't you sit down?'

'All right,' she said. She crossed the room and seated herself.

Only then did she realize that she had crossed that dividing line. She did not have time to analyse her feelings further because he spoke again.

'Are those three Texans still in gaol?'

She started a little at the abrupt question. As she looked up at him he seemed to tower. His one hand brushed his gun. The gun that had killed men. It did not seem strange to her that she felt no fear of him, that she answered his question without a tremor in her voice.

'Yes. Everybody thinks they're in league with you. I've said they're not, but I'm an outsider the same as they, and nobody will listen to me. They just think I'm a cheap dancing girl trying to show-off. I talked to the marshal . . .'

'Yeh? What does he think?'

'Who knows what that man thinks,' she replied with a nervous giggle. 'Maybe he thinks I'm in league with you too.'

'Are you?' he said, and his voice was hardly audible.

She said: 'Well, I wouldn't hand you over to that horrible Craig Jepson, so I suppose I am in a way.'

He was silent for a moment, his side towards her. What he said next was totally unexpected.

'What was that you brought in with you? You dropped it just inside the door.'

He went across and picked up the bedraggled old hat. 'I found it in the grass outside,' she told him.

The sunlight hit his face then: it was immobile but something she saw in his eyes made her suddenly afraid. He took a few more steps to the door and flung

88

the hat outside. Then he turned and crossed to the window and stood looking out.

Her fear went as quickly as it had come and she rose and went across to stand behind him.

They looked out onto the sluggish backwater of Tucson and saw people moving in the street. She became alarmed for him and said, impulsive as ever:

'You must go. You must get away from here. Somebody may have seen me enter here. They may come to investigate . . .'

'Nobody comes near this place,' he said. 'It's haunted. It's bad.' Was it only her fancy or did she detect a note of bitterness in his voice this time.

'You must go,' she said. 'It's silly to stay here. Please go.' She realized that, almost unconsciously, she had grasped his arm.

She let her hands fall and stood away from him a little. He turned to face her. He said:

'I'll go if you promise me something.'

'What?'

'If you'll promise to meet me here at the same time tomorrow morning.'

How strange he was; and a little frightening too. Even so, she knew she must see him again. She nodded her head.

'All right,' she said. 'Now go.'

His hand reached out and gripped hers, pressed it gently. His eyes were shadowed beneath the wide hat brim. Then he was past her.

When she turned he was going through the back door. Presently she followed, and found herself in a little lean-to kitchen. As she stood there she heard the hoof-beats of his horse rapidly fading. When she went to the little window and wiped away the dust she could not see him.

She went out front and mounted her own horse. She rode into the street among the cabins and clapboard shacks. A man sitting on a stoop looked up at her curiously, almost insolently. There was a look on his face very like that in Johnny Salom's, but it was less healthy, more shifty. His feet were bare, his toes wriggled in the dust. She wondered if he was one of the horse-thieves, one of the Salter brothers.

As she rode she realized that Johnny Salom had not told her why he had been waiting in the cabin since dawn.

2

Marshal Lafe Cuthbertson was a widower. He had living quarters over the gaol and his office. A half-breed woman came to give the place a good clean-up every week, but, apart from that, Lafe, being an independent old cuss, catered for himself.

He was frying himself a nice mess of rump steak and onions for supper when heard the sound. Like as if somebody had shoved up the sash of his bedroom window. He deposited the frying-pan and its contents gently where they would not get scorched and took his Colt from the gun-belt on the table beside him. Luckily he had on his moccasins. He padded across the room to the bedroom door, and put his ear to it.

He heard no sound; but still he was not satisfied. He had heard something and he was not the type of man to dismiss it as merely due to cats and not take the trouble to investigate. He gently pressed the latch of the door and held it for a second, listening all the time.

Still he heard no sound from in there. He pushed the door slowly open, and insinuated his big body into the room. He made a sideways movement and leaned against the wall. The window was a grey square opposite him. It was open a little at the bottom, just as he had left it.

He stood regarding it for a moment then began to cross the room towards the lamp on the small table. He heard something behind him and tried to turn. The rim of a gunbarrel jabbed into his back forestalling any more movement. In his old-age Lafe had learned discretion. He did nothing as a hand came around in front of him and gently took his gun. That hard thing in his back was a very effective curb.

'Who are you?' he said.

There was no answer to his question, but a voice said: 'Turn around slowly, marshal.'

He turned and the other man swivelled with him, the gun still remaining at the same position, about an inch to the right hand side of the big man's spine.

'Go back through the door,' said the voice.

The marshal did as he was told and they passed into the lighted room.

'You can turn around now, marshal,' said the voice. 'Sit down on that chair. Take it easy.'

Lafe turned and lowered his bulk into the lumpy

91

horsehair armchair. He looked up at the dark, lean young man before him.

'You're Johnny Salom, I guess,' he said.

'Yeh, I'm Johnny Salom. Glad to meet yuh, marshal. As I've kinda got my hands full I won't shake with yuh.' He hefted the two guns, his own and Lafe's. He sat on the edge of the table and looked down at the lawman. Then he gave a little shrug of his broad shoulders, bolstered his own gun and stuck the other one in his waistband.

'You look a sensible man,' he said. He shrugged again and his gun seemed to leap into his hand.

'I am sensible,' said Lafe, as the younker holstered the gun once more. 'What do you want with me?'

'Conversation,' was the laconic reply.

'Look,' said the marshal. 'I was doin' my supper when you busted in. It's spoilin' while we gab. I hate to see that. You've got me over a barrel; youth on your side, both the guns – cain't I serve my supper up while we talk . . .'

'All right,' said Johnny Salom.

Lafe Cuthbertson rose gingerly, turned, crossed to his stove. Fat was congealing around the steak and onions in the pan. He held them over the jet once more until they hissed and spluttered. For a moment he had a reckless impulse to turn and fling the contents of the pan at the man behind him.

It did not take him more than a split-second to decide that that wasn't such a good idea. The hot fat might find its mark, with terrible effect, but knowing the speed of the Kid's miraculous draw, the old man realized he would not live to see it. He said, over his shoulder:

'There's plenty here for both of us. Would yuh like a plate?'

'I don't mind,' said the Kid.

The marshal put another plate to warm. He filled the one he already had and turned and placed it before his visitor, complete with knife and fork.

'Help yourself to bread,' he said.

Johnny Salom nodded his thanks and set to. A few seconds later the marshal joined him, sitting at the opposite end of the table. Neither of them seemed to see any strangeness in their positions. Through a mouthful of food the older man said:

'Now, what's this conversation you would have with me?'

'I just wanted to tell you a story,' said Johnny Salom.

It was about fifteen minutes later, the plates were mopped clean and pushed aside, and both men were smoking, when the younger man finished talking. His last sentence was:

'What do you think of that, Mr Marshal?'

The other shook his grizzled head. 'Cain't tell you right now,' he said. 'It'll take a lot o' figuring out. How do I know it ain't all moonshine?' He dropped his smoking stub to the floor and ground it thoughtfully beneath his heel.

'You don't know,' said Johnny Salom. 'Turn around, will you, marshal?' The lawman blinked as the muzzle of a gun was pointed at him once more.

'Sorry I gotta do this,' said Johnny Salom. 'It's a poor

93

way to repay your hospitality. I want yuh to understand that there's nothin' personal behind it . . .'

'No,' said the marshal and turned. At a further order from his visitor he pulled his chair away from the table. The young man came around to him.

'I shall have to borrow your belt and neck-cloth,' he said and took them.

He tied the marshal's wrists to the back of the chair with the belt and gagged him with the blue and white neckerchief.

'There,' he said. 'You'll soon wriggle your way outa that. An' nobody's gonna know I ever visited yuh, unless you tell 'em. I'll leave your gun in the other room. My apologies once more for inconveniencing you. And thank you for the supper. You certainly can cook. So-long.'

Lafe Cuthbertson looked up at him as he backed away and the eyes above the gag expressed mingled feelings very hard to define. Then, with a last flip of his hand, Johnny Salom was gone.

The following morning the Yaqui village was visited again by Inch Lemmings. The blocky red-head went through the ritual with the old chief, trying with difficulty to conceal his impatience. He jumped up and grabbed Johnny Salom by the arm as soon as that imperturbable worthy arrived.

'What's eatin' you?' said the young man leading him away.

Inch said: 'The marshal's let them three Texans outa gaol. Insufficient evidence he says. Craig Jepson's hoppin' mad.' The blocky man inclined his head and looked up into the taller man's face. 'Have you bin up to something?'

The Kid said: 'I paid the marshal a visit and talked to him.'

'You talked to him?'

'Yeh, I told him a story.'

'You told him a story?'

'Yeh – a true story. I don't know whether he believed it or not. It appears now that he must've believed some of it.'

'I see what you mean,' said Inch Lemmings, but the look on his face belied his words.

NINE

Annabella Strudel endeavoured to be sane and practical minded. She told herself she was playing with fire in associating with this outlaw, this wanted man. Then again, she told herself she was a cheap little seeker after sensation, interested in this man only because he was handsome and dangerous, an epitome of all the lawless Western fighting men she had ever heard of; that she wasn't interested in him for himself, but was fascinated by his dark and implacable nature.

At times she felt like a moth fascinated by a flame, knowing that if she persisted she would get badly burnt. Then she resolved never to see him again, not to keep her rendezvous as she had promised. The night before she told herself that. But when the morning came she knew she would go: as she began her usual routine she knew that her touch on the horse's reins would inevitably lead him to that tumbledown cabin beside the creek. And she knew that she was interested in Johnny Salom, not for what he had been and what folks said he was now, but for how he appeared to her. He did not need her pity or help, but, somehow, she knew he needed her friendship. If not, why had he asked her to come?

This time she was more cautious: she rode her mount behind the hut before dismounting from him. She entered by the front door, stooping so that she was almost hidden by the long grass before she passed into the dim, sun-barred interior.

She had expected to see him there, and was disappointed when she realized the place was empty. She sat down on the rickety chair, and, with her hands in her lap, composed herself to wait.

The sun-bar widened and touched the toe of her shoes. She saw the dust on the mildewed boards of the floor. Thick, grey dust in which she could faintly discern her own footmarks.

Time dragged greyly like the dust and her spirits dragged with it. He wasn't coming. She was a fool. The best thing she could do was to get up and go out and ride away and forget all about him. Then years later she could remember how she had almost kept an assignation with a notorious 'killer' and contemplate with a shudder how narrow her escape had been.

She realized she was not amused by such fancies, that they could not dispel her gloom as the time passed, that she wanted to see him and must wait a little longer, still a little longer, in case he came . . . Perhaps he could not come. Perhaps they had caught him. Perhaps . . . perhaps . . . tiny wings of fear beat in the recesses of her mind.

She could not suppress a cry of alarm as a step sounded behind her. She whirled. She had not heard his horse hoofs, had not heard him enter. But he was there.

He took her hand as she rose. 'I'm sorry I startled you,' he said. 'Coming in out of the sunshine I did not see you at first, you were sitting so still and quiet.'

'I thought you weren't coming,' she said.

Then he dropped her hand and they were both silent. He seemed ill at ease – a state which she had thought was foreign to his nature. Taciturn, yes, even surly – but always so sure of himself he had seemed to be.

She turned fully towards him in her chair; it seemed to her that he wanted to say something. But still he remained silent. He even turned away from her and wandered over towards the window. He was etched against the light, straight as an arrow, his profile bent a little beneath the wide brim of the sombrero, his one hand hooked in his belt, the other hanging lax at his side. His legs were a little apart, with one knee bent. The attitude was negligent yet there was a hint of tense watchfulness about it, and she thought, with a sudden spasm of pity, of how for him there was no peace, he was doomed to eternal vigilance.

His flat, soft voice cut in on her thoughts. He said:

'I was born here, so I'm told. I lived here with my mother. She was what people called a bad woman. But she was good to me. I can never remember her ever doing anybody any harm . . .'

The girl was moved to remark: 'I know. I would liked to have known her. I think we should have understood each other . . .'

He went on almost as if she had not spoken, his soft

98

words like a spoken reverie.

'She was the only woman I ever had any truck with. Sometimes it seemed like we were just pals instead of mother an' son. She was the only woman who ever took any interest in me . . .'

She expected him to say "except you", but if he had intended to, the sentence remained unspoken. What a fool she was . . .

His mind seemed to have gone on the same tack for he said:

'Why am I telling you all this? It's of no interest to you . . .'

'But it is,' she retorted. 'You tell me all you wish . . .'

'I guess you know most of it,' he said, his voice rising a little. 'How I was always in trouble. The bad boy of Tucson, the outcast, the unwashed. Of how I finally killed two men and went to gaol . . . I had to kill them. They were armed. It was me or them. They were . . .' He suddenly stopped.

Her head was bent. She was looking at the floor, building up in her mind the picture his voice evoked. There was no bitterness in the flat tones of his voice, but she could build bitterness up in her mind. She said: 'Go on, Johnny,' realizing, but without shame, that she had called him, for the first time, by his name.

Still he remained silent and she looked up and at him. His position was markedly tense now and he was looking away from her. As she watched he took three cat-like steps to the window. His hand dropped to the butt of his gun. He remained motionless like that as he looked out.

She rose silently and went up behind him. Then her fist flew to her mouth in that old gesture of alarm. A band of horsemen had left the end of the street and was making straight for the hut. She recognized Marshal Cuthbertson, Craig Jepson, Inch Lemmings; other well-known Tucson fighting men. It was a grim-looking posse.

Johnny Salom drew his gun. She caught hold of his shoulder.

'No,' she said. 'Go, while you still have a chance.'

He turned about, almost knocking her over. Then, as he passed her, his eyes met hers and she recoiled from what she saw in them.

She was stunned for a moment, then, as he went through the kitchen doorway, she ran after him crying.

'No, Johnny. No, I didn't, Johnny. I didn't.'

She heard the soft thud of the closing back door and she halted in her stride. She was trembling. She heard his horse start up, break into a gallop. There was a fusilade of shots, the thunder of more hoofs, the whole blending into a crescendo of sound.

Something broke within her and she leaned her temple against the jamb of the door and began to sob, saying 'Johnny, Johnny,' softly over and over again. And all around her now was a dead empty silence.

2

As the Yaqui Kid rode there was murder in his heart. His gun was still in his hand but he did not turn and fire at his pursuers because he knew his friend, Inch, was among them. A few scattered slugs winged after him and looking back, he saw that his blocky red-headed friend was riding in front with Marshal Cuthbertson. The old lawman was too canny to waste shots: all the letting off of guns was being done by Craig Jepson and a few of his minions, although the markedly erratic riding of Inch Lemmings spoiled their aim more than somewhat. Despite his fury the Yaqui Kid could hardly suppress a tight smile.

His horse was a fleet paint Indian and probably faster than those behind. If he did not get a slug in his back or run into something up ahead he had a good chance of escape. No thanks to the woman back in the cabin, he reflected grimly.

It was characteristic of him that after that last grim thought he forgot the past and concentrated on the speeding present, lying low over his pony's neck as he urged it to greater efforts. The beast, who was used to having other horses at its heels and bullets buzzing around it, responded nobly. Johnny Salom's dark face became almost animated as he felt the silk muscles ripple beneath him, as the beast, finding a reserve of strength from some unknown source, increased its stride.

Pretty soon he was out in the badlands. Bunches of mesquite, sage and greasewood flashed past him or were scaled by the flying hoofs. The blue peaks of the mountains were before him. The peaceful green mesa and the cottonwoods were left behind and he was in the savage country that was friendly to such as he. It had its beauty too, a wild beauty that suited him, flashing by in multicoloured tints of land and sky. He was the hunted, the outcast desert-wolf; the hunters were on his heels, and, in this land, it seemed right that that should be so.

Among the fantastic rock formations of the foothills the pursuers lost him. They halted, casting about to try and pick up his trail.

Craig Jepson said: 'The devil's given us the slip again. He knows this territory like the back of his hand.'

The saloon-man's voice was shaking with rage, a little incoherent as he went on . . . 'If we could've got to the cabin earlier . . . He must have seen us – or the girl did . . . The girl was there we know that . . . The vixen's helping him, making a fool of us all . . . I'll turn her out of my place . . . She's a spy, I won't have her around my place any more . . .'

Marshal Cuthbertson said: 'I thought you'd signed a contract with the whole troupe to stay with you a month. She's their leader. You can't break contract an' turn her out, can you. . . ?'

Jepson glared at the marshal, knowing that what he said was true. 'You ought to lock her up,' he flared again.

'Lockin' the girl up won't help to catch the Yaqui Kid.'

'I'll have her watched all the time she's in my place.'

'You do that,' said the marshal solemnly.

'Looks like he came through here,' said one of the tracking men suddenly.

'What are we waiting for, then?' said Cuthbertson. 'Get mounted. Let's get after him again.'

They negotiated a narrow pass that led right through

the hills out on to the arid land beyond the 'badlands' proper – and very worthy of the title they were too.

It was then the sound came to them, a deliberate pulse-beat filling the air all around them. They reined in once more.

'Injun drums,' said Inch Lemmings. 'Yaquis most probably. The Apaches are gettin' too damn educated to hold festivities . . .'

'They're not war-drums?' said another man.

'Nah,' said Inch with a pitying shake of his head at such ignorance. 'Joy-drums. Feast-drums. It must be the beginning of their season of festivities; they start about this time . . .'

'Primitive rites,' said the other man.

'Yeh, I guess so. The Yaquis are proud that they have not given way to the white man's influence. I've heard that these big shindigs they have this time of the year are almost religious. They do plays about the fight between good and evil. They dress up as 'bad coyotes' and 'good deers'. I guess there ain't many white men know the full story. The Yaquis are mighty touchy about spies at times like these. Any white man caught snooping is consigned to the flames pronto.'

Although Inch spoke mainly in order to try and dissuade his companions from approaching the village, there was no moonshine in his tale, it was all true. He knew that even he who was known to these people, would risk his life if he tried to invade their territory while the ceremonial dances were in progress.

'Come on,' said Marshal Cuthbertson. 'Ain't it feasible that a *hombre* who's known as the Yaqui Kid is likely to be somewhere around a Yaqui village ? A lot of drum-thumpin' ain't gonna make me turn back.'

They rode on and pretty soon could see the Yaqui village in the valley. They descended to the level then slackened their horses' pace, advancing on the place with peaceable mein. The beat of the drums seemed to shake the very earth beneath them.

'There's a bunch of them coming,' said Craig Jepson.

'Keep movin,' said the marshal.

The Indians came on at about the same pace. Many of them were in full regalia: feathered head-dresses, short, gaily decorated vests which left their arms and chests bare. Their skin was painted in complicated patterns with white pigment and they had strings of wampum around their necks. One or two of the most gaily decorated wore hideous masks with curly horns or upstanding ears. There were about twenty braves in all and a good percentage of them carried long feathered lances. They sat erect in their saddles with their weapons held aloft. There was no haste about their pace or the way they carried themselves, but there was something implacable, and a little nerve-wracking to the white men, about their approach.

As they drew nearer both Inch Lemmings and Marshal Cuthbertson raised their hands in salute. There were no answering motions from the approaching Yaquis.

They drew steadily nearer. They were about a hundred yards away when Craig Jepson drew his gun.

Luckily the marshal spotted the movement and

reached back urgently with his hand.

'Put that away, you fool,' he snarled.

The untempered virulence of the command shocked the saloon-man into obeying it with instinctive speed.

Inch Lemmings blew out a sudden gust of breath. 'Any more movements like that an' we'll have the whole village on our necks,' he said. 'I don't think they noticed that one.'

'You know the lingo better'n any of us I guess,' said the marshal. 'You talk to 'em.'

'All right,' said Inch. 'I'd like you to stay here, all of yuh.'

The marshal seemed reluctant to do so but after a spasm of conjecture, gave the word. Inch continued on alone and, as he approached them, the Indians reined in their mounts.

The posse watched as Inch stopped directly in front of the awesome bunch of braves and raised his hand in salute once more. This time it was answered and a befeathered Yaqui edged his horse a little way from the others, confronting Inch, with his lance held upright beside him.

'I don't like the look o' them pig-stickers,' said Lafe Cuthbertson.

'Cain't we do nothin' ?' said Craig Jepson. 'The Kid might be skulking back there laughing at us.'

'This is a ticklish situation,' said Cuthbertson. 'Wait for Inch.'

All the while they were talking the drums beat on, their focal point the round cluster of tepees, spreading from there with echoing vibrations which shook the ground and vibrated in the air all around.

Inch Lemmings was talking to the tall Indian who had moved away from his fellows. They made gestures with their hands. Inch pointed towards the village, the Indian pointed in the other direction, making a sweeping motion with a brown, painted arm. Watching them, the small group of white men were tense and nervous.

Finally the Indian retreated into the ranks of his party and the whole bunch of them remained motionless as Inch Lemmings turned his horse and rode back to the posse. He said:

'As I thought, they don't take kindly to our intrusion. That *hombre* I talked to is one of the younger chiefs. He says that if we keep a-comin' he won't answer for the consequences. The Yaquis don't like white men snooping in on their traditional dances – I guess they were going on long before an Injun saw the first paleface – they're liable to resent us in a manner that would be painful, and, maybe permanent, to us. While the festivities are on they want no truck with white men. That chief tells me he ain't seen a white man in months . . .'

'The Kid's skulking in there,' burst out Craig Jepson. 'They're shielding him . . .'

'If that Injun says he ain't seen a white man, he ain't,' said Inch. 'It stands to commonsense that they wouldn't even let Johnny Salom in on thet shindig. It'd be a kind of sacrilege.'

'D'yuh think he's gone past there?' said the marshal. Inch shook his head. 'If he did they'd've seen him. They spotted us quick enough. An' he hadn't enough start on us to have time to make a wide detour, we'd've

106

spotted him ourselves. No, I think he's hiding back in the hills there. We've passed him somehow . . .'

'That's what I'm beginning to think,' said Cuthbertson, turning his horse. 'C'mon, let's, git movin'.'

Even the peevish Jepson seemed to see the logic of this step. The sight of the implacable group of Indians a hundred or so yards away was beginning to make his blood freeze.

As they rode back Inch Lemmings' mind was full of reflections. He hoped he had done right by putting the posse on to the track in the hills. It was true the tall Indian chief had told him he had seen no white man. Inch believed that. He realized that the man did not belong to that particular village but, it being feast time, had probably come on a visit to the old chief. Consequently he would not know Johnny Salom. Even if the Kid was in hiding there now it was quite probable that the tall Yaqui had not seen him.

Although Inch had stressed the fact that no white man was allowed to see the legendary Yaqui dances, which was quite true, he knew that Johnny Salom, reputed to have Indian blood himself, and who was also a 'blood-brother' of the old chiefs would not be debarred. In fact, he could take part in the dancing and, strange creature that he was, probably did.

The white men looked back and saw that the Indians were riding back to the village. The drums beat incessantly with a steady, sinister pulse.

TEN

The posse did not find the Yaqui Kid or any sign of him among the hills, and, with weary failure behind them once more and frustration in more than one heart, returned to Tucson. There, evading questions as much as possible, they split up; Craig Jepson to his apartments above the Golden Wheel, the marshal to his office, Inch Lemmings to the blacksmith's shop, the others to resume their lounging or their occupations.

Jepson was met at the bottom of his stairs by two men. They were both lean and young, with long faces and shifty eyes. They could almost have been twins. They were at least brothers. They were dressed very much alike, in battered felt hats, colourless open-neck shirts, canvas trousers, moccasins. They wore their guns hanging low and each had a knife tucked into his belt for good measure. One of them had a distinguishing mark in the shape of a long, jagged white scar down his cheek. It was he who spoke in a husky, whining drawl.

'It didn't come off, Mr Jepson?'

'No, it didn't come off. He gave us the slip again. You

ought to've gotten him while you had the chance.'

'We wuz kinda leary 'cos o' the gel . . .'

Jepson waved an impatient hand: 'Where is she?'

'She came back. We follered her. She's up in her room now.'

'All right. I want both of you to hang around. Josh, I want you to come up with me and stay in the passage. Keep an eye on the girl's room and on the backstairs. If she goes out follow her. If you have to scare her do so. Maybe she'll go a-running to her precious Yaqui Kid.'

'All right, Mr Jepson,' said the scar-faced one.

Jepson turned to the other. 'Ike, you stay down here and keep your eyes open – particularly if any Texans come snooping around. If Josh needs any help you help him. And not too much liquor, you understand.'

'All right, Mr Jepson. You c'n trust me.'

'You boys stick by me and you're on a good thing. We'll nail the Yaqui Kid's scalp over our door before he's much older.'

'You betcha,' said Josh as he followed the saloon-owner up the stairs.

Ike waited till they had disappeared then he went over to the bar. The barman looked at him suspiciously and continued to polish glasses.

'Gimme a whiskey,' said Ike, and threw a crumpled bill on the bar-top.

The barman eyed it with disfavour and then gave Ike a dark look from under lowered brows.

'Gimme a whiskey,' said Ike again, and his shifty eyes flamed, his face twisted a little.

The barman shrugged, reached behind him for a

bottle and glass, and poured a tot. He took the bill and went away with it. Returning with the change he plonked it down on the bar with unnecessary emphasis.

Ike took the drink over to a table by the corner. From there he could watch the sunlit street.

Annabella Strudel left her room. She was the only member of the troupe who stayed at the Golden Wheel. A guest of honour, she had been, but now the hospitality seemed to have soured on her. She decided to go down to the boarding-house where the rest of the girls stayed, a bit of lightheartedly malicious feminine companionship was just what she needed. Her heart was heavy and her nerves jumpy. Also there were things she wanted to find out. Staying in her room would not help. If they had caught Johnny surely the news would be shouted from the housetops.

A man stood in the passage outside. He was leaning against the door of the backstairs. He eyed her insolently. She had an idea that he was not one of Craig Jepson's regular hands but that nevertheless she had seen him somewhere before. She turned away from him and could not resist giving a little flounce of her skirts. What did he mean by standing there as if he owned the place, and staring at her almost as if he owned her too? It was a pity, but so many men had that kind of an idea about dancing girls.

She heard his footsteps and, as she reached the top of the stairs, looked back. She was a little disconcerned to discover that he was following her – or at least he was walking behind her. After that she kept her head high and looked straight ahead as she descended the stairs and crossed the bar-room. It was empty except for the barman and an early drinker at a table by the window. She noticed that the former did not call out his customary greeting. She was in Coventry, no doubt, she thought, with a little burst of cynicism. She passed through the batwings into the sunshine. She turned left, her heels going clack-clack on the boardwalk.

Thudding footsteps sounded behind her and, before she could stop herself, she had glanced over her shoulder once more. The lean, seedy man was still behind her. There seemed little doubt that he was indeed following her. Was he a lawman? He did not look like one.

The rhythmical clang of a heavy hammer striking steel came to her as she drew near the blacksmith's shop. Then the sound ceased, and, as she drew abreast with the warm dark maw of the doorway, Inch Lemmings came out and almost ran into her.

He drew up short, his hand flying to the brim of his hat.

'I'm sorry, Miss Strudel,' he said.

'It's quite all right.'

He smiled and his ruddy face became suddenly full of gentle good-humour. It was hard to think that he was one of the men who had hounded Johnny Salom. Still, she reflected, he and many other good men thought they were in the right in doing so – maybe they were! On an impulse she spoke quickly:

'Did you catch the Yaqui Kid?'

His smile died but his voice was gentle as he replied:

'No, Miss Strudel, we didn't.' There was a look in his eyes that baffled her as he added. 'We never shall.' The words seemed so strange coming from him.

She looked over her shoulder again. Her follower was leaning against a hitching-rail a few yards away.

She said to Inch: 'Who is that man behind?'

He did not stare. He merely replied: 'That's Josh, one o' the Salter brothers. What's he doin' this end o' town...?'

'He was upstairs by my room. He followed me down here.'

'Oh, he did, did he?' Inch paused for a moment. Then he said: 'You carry on to wherever you were goin', Miss Strudel. I'll keep an eye on Josh...'

'I don't want to cause any trouble, Mr Lemmings. I...'

'That's all right, gel. I'll just keep an eye on him, that's all. You go on.'

With a little bow of her head in consent she went on. As she climbed the steps to the boarding-house she looked back. Her lean follower was still in evidence but there was no sign of Mr Lemmings. A puzzled frown overclouded her smooth brow, but she quelled it as her friends – they would never let her down – called out gay greetings.

2

She was in a happier frame of mind when she left the place almost an hour later. Her spirits sank when saw her follower leaning against a wall on the other side of the street. Still, maybe she was making mountains out of molehills: she turned resolutely away from him and set off along the boardwalk towards the Golden Wheel.

As she approached the blacksmith's shop she looked for Mr Lemmings. But he was nowhere in sight. Her lips curled a little. She looked over her shoulder. Yes, the lean man was on her trail.

She passed the blacksmith's and went on. The padding footsteps came at an even pace behind. Then, quite suddenly, they stopped.

She turned her head. Between her and her follower now was the blocky form of Inch Lemmings. He was bareheaded and his red hair glinted as the sun caught it. His one hand was making little movements at his side as he talked to Josh Salter. She saw Josh scowl, his mouth leering as he spoke back.

She halted, stepping back a little into the shadow of an adobe wall. She saw Josh Salter start to come on once more and Inch Lemmings block his path. She saw the lean man's face go white, his scar standing out on it, livid in the sunlight. Her hand flew up to her mouth in the old gesture. What would they do? What could she do? She began to move back towards them.

Out of the corner of his eye Inch saw her.

'Stay where you are, Miss Strudel,' he said.

The cold authority of his voice lashed her to a standstill. She realized that, at a time like this, these Western men wanted no interference. She wanted to call out to Mr Lemmings, but knew she must not. If they fought, oh, let him win, let him win!

Josh Salter had stopped moving. His face was still

white, set, but his eyes were shiftier than ever. Annabella hoped it was fear she saw glittering there.

She heard footsteps behind her. Padding, sliding footsteps. Slowly she turned her head. A man was coming from the Golden Wheel, and as she saw him plainly she felt a shock that made her tremble. He was so like Josh Salter. Almost a twin except for the scar. She knew without a doubt that this was the other Salter brother.

His black eyes were fixed on Inch Lemmings' back and he did not seem to see her in the shadows. She flattened herself against the wall. The light in those black eyes was unmistakable. That was why he did not see her. His gaze, not shifty now, but a little glazed, was fixed on the back of the man he meant to kill.

She looked at Inch and Josh, her tongue cleaving to the roof of her mouth as she got ready to shout. Then things began to happen.

Josh's hand suddenly streaked for his gun. Inch's arm came up, the elbow crooked. The fist sank into the lean man's middle. She saw Josh's mouth shoot open, his eyes pop. Both hands came around in front of him. Then the man nearest Annabella went for his gun and she screamed: 'Mr Lemmings, look out!'

Inch whirled, throwing himself sideways. At the same instant Annabella threw herself flat on the floor. She heard the boom of a gun and there was a queer screaming sound above her. Slivers of wood and shining bits of steel fell near her.

A voice boomed: 'Hold it, everybody!'

Slowly she raised her head and looked about her.

114

The brother nearest to her had his hand on his gun but he was not doing anything with it. Inch Lemmings was leaning against the wall. His gun was out, but there was no smoke coming from the muzzle. Josh was on his hands and knees, and, as she watched, he began to rise. All of them seemed to be looking across the street.

A man broke away from the shadows across there by the print shop. A little fat man with a bald head that gleamed in the sunlight. Jebb Downs, editor of the *Tucson Herald*. And in his hands he held a sawn-off shotgun, from the muzzle of which blue smoke lazily curled.

Annabella rose slowly to her feet, and for the first time the little printer seemed to see her.

His mouth dropped open. 'Gosh,' he said. 'I nearly killed yuh, miss. I didn't see anybody near this snake.' He indicated the second brother with a jerk of his head that made the bald pate flash.

'I'm all right,' said Annabella, shakily. 'I'm glad you did fire. This man was going to shoot Mr Lemmings in the back.'

'That's Ike's speciality,' said Jebb Downs. 'Take your mitt away from that shooter, Ike.'

Ike showed his yellow teeth in a snarl like a trapped animal, but he did not speak. And he took his hand off his shooter.

His brother Josh was on his feet now. He said: 'That wuz a fool play, Mr Editor.'

'It was,' agreed Jebb. 'Inasmuch that I didn't fill yuh both with slugs while I had the chance. Move up here.'

'Do as he says,' said Inch Lemmings and prodded Josh with his gun. Josh moved up.

Inch said: 'Thanks, Jeb. Looks like you saved my bacon.'

'Mebbe,' said the little editor. 'Though by the speed o' that draw I figure you'd got a good chance – even against the pair of them. I didn't know you were that fast.'

'I ain't a shootin' man.'

'Nope, but you certainly handled yourself like one that time.'

People were beginning to filter into the street, among them Inch's partner, old stalwart black-bearded Josh Cornfield, complaining querulously about being woken from his after-dinner nap.

'Time you woke up, yuh old coot,' Inch told him. 'If nothing wakes yuh that after-dinner nap of yours is liable to last till the follering mawnin'.'

At this juncture Marshal Cuthbertson hove in sight, a sturdy frigate in full sail; and with a scowl beneath his moustache which promised ill for whoever was disturbing the peace. He had enough trouble with the Yaqui Kid without the townsfolk letting off guns at each other.

He saw Jeb Downs with the still-smoking shotgun and barked: 'What in tarnation are yuh doin' with that?'

'Just preventin' a man from getting shot in the back,' was the imperturbable reply. 'Or ain't that a right thing to do?'

'I guess it is. Who was tryin' to shoot who in the back?' Then the marshal spotted the Salter brothers. 'Oh,' he said. 'You two buzzards are here, are yuh.'

'We got a right to be any place in town,' said Josh. 'We've lived here all our lives. We don't need no tin-pot lawman to tell us what to do.'

The marshal seemed to control himself with an effort. He turned once more to Jeb. 'Speak your piece,' he said. Jeb told him of what he had seen through the open door of the print shop. He had almost finished when Ike Salter chimed in with:

'Lemmings hit Josh while he wasn't looking. He never had a chance . . .'

The blocky red-head opened his lips to speak but a shriller voice beat him:

'It's a lie. He went for his gun. Mr Lemmings hit him. Then, this man,' jerking a gloved hand in Ike's direction, 'tried to shoot him in the back. Mr Lemmings stopped the scar-faced man for me because he's bin following me around town all morning.'

'What yuh listenin' to her fer,' snarled Ike suddenly. 'She's only Johnny Salom's fancy woman.'

Inch Lemmings and the marshal both started forward, but the girl beat them to it. Her gloved hand landed on Ike's check with a resounding smack. Ike staggered back, his hand instinctively reaching for his gun once more. The marshal, surprisingly agile for all his age and bulk, tripped him with an outstretched foot.

When Ike scrambled to his feet his gun was in the big man's hand. Inch Lemmings had also relieved brother Josh of his. He prodded him along until he stood beside Ike. Cuthbertson said:

'Let's hear yuh sing. Why were you follerin' Miss Strudel?'

Josh's eyes dropped, the cur in him became uppermost. In a whining voice he said:

'Mr Jepson tol' me to. We're both workin' for him now.'

'Oh, you are, are you?' snarled Cuthbertson. 'All right, turn around an' march! We'll see Mr Jepson about this. I ain't havin' no damn hoss-thieves embarrassing ladies in the streets o' Tucson. Go on, you coyotes. Move!'

The two men began to shuffle forward.

'I'll come along with yuh,' said Inch Lemmings and fell into step beside the marshal.

'I guess I will too,' said Jeb Downs. He held out a crooked arm to Annabella, and said with a chubby grin: 'Will you walk along with me, Miss Strudel?'

The girl took his arm gladly and they brought up the rear of the cavalcade. She was very grateful to the little editor, who, understandingly, had joshed her out of the sick despondency Ike Salter's insulting remark had engendered in her. She knew Ike's words had not been resented by everyone, judging by the suspicious or downright venonmous glances that were thrown at her. She had a cold feeling in the pit of the stomach, wondering what form the animosity of these loungers would take were she not under the protection of this little fat man, his shotgun, and his friends.

ELEVEN

All night the dancing and miming had gone on around the huge fire in the centre of the village, as one batch of men dropped out, exhausted, to sleep on the ground within the circle, others took their places. The drummers worked in relays too, no man taking his rythmically beating hands from the tight skin until his relief had his there and got into the exact swing of the beat. The rhythm remained unbroken, unaltered, incessant.

As dawn began to flush the Arizona skies the beat slackened a little, the tempo changed, something brooding and ominous about it. It was a sign that the grand tableau was due to begin. All eyes were turned on the venerable old chief who was to give the final signal.

He sat on his throne, the packing-case laid with soft skins. Because of his age he had waived tradition and the ceremony and finery that went with it. He was still clad in his old rusty serape, his monkey-like, calloused bare feet showing below it. A vee of his scrawny chest showed too, and he did not even have a necklace of

119

wampum around his neck. A single feather drooped in his long, greasy hair, which was a dull, dark silver.

Around him sat the younger, lesser chiefs, members of his own tribe as well as others come to visit this new site the old man had chosen for the village in which he meant to spend the last days of his life. On the left-hand side of him, squatting cross-legged on a brilliantly-woven carpet was another figure in a serape. A young man with a lean, dark face, almost hidden by the wide-brimmed sombrero he wore so that not everybody there realized that he was a white man. The bottom of buckskin trousers and a pair of moccasins showed beneath the folds of his coat, and around his neck, so bronzed that it was like any Indians, was a string of brightly coloured wampum. To the Yaquis who moved around incessantly, excited by the festivities, it seemed like a young brave who wore a white man's hat had been sitting there by the chief ever since the festivities began, although in reality, he had only taken his place there just before noon yesterday. Last night he had stretched out within the fringes of the firelit circle like many others and slept on his blanket there. Only the favoured members of the tribe knew that he was Johnny Salom. They called him 'Pascola', which means 'good fighting man' (the 'good' in this instance standing for 'just' and 'right') but to other white men he was known as the Yaqui Kid.

The old chief suddenly clapped his shrivelled hands together. Because of the drums nobody heard the sound they made, but everybody whose business it was to watch, saw the movement. And the traditional ceremony began – in the same form it had taken centuries ago when the red men owned the great plains and the desert and had never seen a face of a different colour to their own. Other Redskins had fought and had been conquered and had adopted, or bastardized to their own needs the ways of the white men, but the Yaquis, a small peace-loving set, had clung to their old customs and beliefs.

Into the arena pranced a cavalcade of dancers wearing doe-skin head-dresses with little ears and horns. They were the deer-dancers, the 'good' people. They danced round and round the fire: there was no wild passion in their movements, only a gentle rhythm.

Suddenly another bunch ran shrieking into the arena. They wore hideously painted masks with long snouts and ears and carried long staves and flat sticks sharpened like swords and covered with painted designs.

They were the 'bad' people, the coyote and wolf dancers, and the deer-men fled before them with terrified cries. They chased them, slashing out with their sticks and swords until every one of the good people were driven away. Then the grotesque evil ones did their wild dance around the fire and the air was hideous with their cries as the drums beat faster and faster.

Then, with dramatic suddenness, the drums slackened their speed again, and a cry went up from the crowd as the deer-dancers began to filter back into the arena. With them came other dancers, bronzed bucks, the pick of the tribe, with gleaming naked torsoes and no finery except for strings of tiny bells around their waists and at their wrists and ankles which jingled as they walked. They were the good fighting men who watched over the deer-dancers, and had come to drive the evil ones away.

The coyotes and wolves put up a show of resistance but were driven back by sticks and missiles. The latter consisted of bundles of dried leaves which were snatched from convenient piles and flung at the evil dancers, until, with shrill terrified cries, they fled in disorder. The drums began to beat faster again and the deer-dancers and their 'good' soldiers did a dance of joy and victory.

Very few people noticed that the serape-clad young man who had sat at the left-hand side of the old chief was no longer there. Maybe more people noticed that one of the stalwart fighting men who had driven away the evil ones was lighter-skinned than any of his brothers. But he danced as well; he was a fine figure of a young buck and his bells jingled merrily.

The miming went on and on, and as the blazing ball of the sun began to reach its zenith, the dancers became bedewed with sweat, panting and wild-eyed. The bad dancers came again and again and were continually driven back. And so it continued until the old chief gave the signal for the culminating triumph of the festivities.

The dancers withdrew and a trio of young bucks carried a thick heavy stake into the arena and placed it upright in a hole which had already been made a few yards away from the blazing fire-pile. They filled the hole in quickly, stamping the earth around the post hard with their moccasined feet.

Delighted cries went up from the crowd as two more bucks carried a huge, hideously-painted effigy into the arena and tied it to the stake with rawhide. Children grabbed bundles of leaves, sticks and stones and ran into the arena to throw at the thing at the stake, the epitome of all bad spirits, the Evil One incarnate. Then all the dancers began to come back into the arena and pranced around the effigy. Many of them carried torches now, and, one by one, they flung them at the figure until it was ringed with flame.

It became a blazing pyre, sending up pungent clouds of black smoke and everybody began to dance with joy and freedom.

The young man in the serape and the big hat had taken up his place beside the old chief once more and sat watching impassively. Only the glitter of his eyes in the shadows of the hat-brim and the tiny crystals of sweat which beaded his face betrayed his interest and the part he had taken in the festivities.

An Indian lad with startled eyes came before them and spoke rapidly, pointing out from the village with a slim hand. Both the old man and the young raised their heads. Then they exchanged glances and the former nodded. The man in the serape and tall hat rose and followed the youth.

The latter took him out beyond the dancing circle and among the empty tepees to the edge of the village. There, surrounded by a hostile group of armed braves, was Inch Lemmings. He started forward when he saw

Johnny Salom but was thrust back by a muscular arm.

The Indian youth spoke a few rapid words and the Yaqui Kid backed him up with slower ones. Throwing final distrustful looks back at Inch, the bucks moved away into the village. The youth went with them, leaving the two white men alone.

Inch said: 'So you were here all the time?'

The other nodded. Then he said: 'I didn't expect you this soon. Especially while this shindig was on. You took a big risk.'

'I had to see yuh. Things are boilin' up in town.'

'Boilin' up? That's how I want 'em to be. What's happening now?'

'What's happening is mainly on account o' that dancing-girl, Annabella Strudel . . .'

'Why? She's a dutiful citizen. She tried to get me taken . . .'

'That's just what she didn't do, yuh dern fool. It was Josh Salter who did that. He wuz spyin' on both of yuh. He was after the reward. Craig Jepson has hired him an' his brother as kind of unofficial bodyguards . . .'

'So I was wrong about the girl,' said Johnny Salom, half to himself. 'I did her a great injustice.'

'You certainly did if you thought she turned you in. Craig Jepson thinks she's in league with you, she's spying on him for you. He had Josh Salter trailin' her yestiddy. I cut up rough about it. There wuz quite a shindig.'

Briefly he told the Kid all that had occurred. Of how Jepson, when confronted by the marshal, Jebb Downs and Inch, with the disgruntled Salter brothers in tow, was very unco-operative and said he was only protecting his own interests. He said maybe he was mistaken about Miss Strudel but that she had definitely met the Yaqui Kid more than once. The Salters were now his men, he needed men like that if this outlaw was after his bood. They were quite right in keeping an eye on the girl, she was a suspicious character – everybody in town said so. The girl wanted to leave but three friends persuaded her to stay. 'It wasn't hard – she's purty worried about you, Johnny,' said Inch. 'She's still at the Golden Wheel 'cos there ain't no room for her at the boarding-house with the rest of the girls.

'Things've bin happenin' mighty fast since then,' he went on. 'We found out – me an' the marshal – that Jepson's plannin' on leaving Tucson. Suddenly, like that, cuttin' his losses an' pullin' up stakes and leavin' – any day now, I guess. He's closed the mine down – after makin' sure its scraped dry – an' we found out from ol' Lynecote, the banker, that he's drawn all his remaining money out. All that he had invested too. Lynecote as well as bein' his banker, is his legal adviser. Jepson's selling all his property too, as fast as he can get rid of it. Seems like he's been doin' that for quite a bit. Jasper Lynecote's a pompous ol' buzzard but he's straight. An' he don't like Jepson. Of late he's beginning to think there's something mighty fishy about him. The marshal's gettin' leary too. You must've talked to him good that night you busted in on him. He figures that if Jepson's got right on his side why is he running away like this – an' he certainly *appears* to be runnin' away . . .'

'He's milked Tucson dry an' now he's pulling out before something blows up in his face,' said Johnny Salom. 'But it's too soon for my likin'. I've got no proof against him an' if he leaves this territory I might never get it. I can follow him wherever he goes. I can kill him. But that ain't enough. I gotta make him talk. I gotta do it now too, it seems . . .'

'But how?'

'I shall need your help.'

'You've got it, you know that. An' that of the others who'll stick by yuh.'

'I want to be sure of those others.'

'I'll make sure for you an' let you know. Then what do you want me to do?'

'I'll tell you,' said the Yaqui Kid.

2

Night had fallen on that arid plain on the edge of the Arizona badlands. The Yaqui village was quiet and still. There was no moon and the stars were very high, casting only a gentle eerie glow over an ancient country which had seen many wierd rites and much bloodshed.

The village was sunk in lethargy after the gruelling finale to the festivities. It looked almost like a ghost-town out on the plains there beneath the blue vault and the myriad stars. But the illusion was dispelled by the figure of a horseman that broke away from the shadowy-cluster and crawled out like a fly on the huge plate of the mesa. He set his horse at a gallop, streaking for the hills. Pretty soon he vanished among them.

About half-an-hour later he appeared again on the shining apex of the highest point of the hills. He sat his horse motionless so that the two of them blended together looking like a carven figure, part and symbol of the wild landscape. He was looking out towards Tucson. From where he sat he could see the tiny pin-points of light glittering there.

The eerie starlight caught his face and etched it like bronze, lean and smooth beneath the big hat, a sheen on the high cheekbones. Suddenly he rose in the saddle.

At a point a little divided from the cluster of lights which was Tucson another light had begun to blossom. It spread rapidly, the red glow of it reflected in the sky.

Any observer could have told it was a quick-bursting fire but to that horseman on the hills it was something else.

It was his old life, his old wasted life burning away before him. It was the cabin in which he was born, destroyed for him by his best friend. Those flames were a symbol.

They were also a signal. Maybe a signal marking the beginning of a new life and maybe a signal marking the end of it all, heralding his death. As he urged his horse down the slope of the hills he knew that, though his destiny was in his own hands, there were many chances he must take before he could fulfil it.

As he rode hard towards the lights of Tucson the fire was beginning to die down. The first part of his plan had been put into operation. He was taking his part, the main role and, as he sped onwards to his destiny, he could only hope that everything was still going right. The fire had been the signal to start it all but now he could only trust in the efficiency and luck of others until he got into Tucson himself.

As he rode into the backwater of the town and tethered his horse in a convenient clump of cottonwoods the fire had died altogether and he could hear the voices of the people in the streets. He was taking chances all the time as he ran along in the blackness of the 'backs' and climbed a fence.

Then once more he was in the alley beside the Golden Wheel, leaning against the wall and listening to the incessant murmur of voices from inside.

People passed to and fro across the dimly lighted oblong which was the end of the alley but, back here in the dim darkness, everything seemed quiet. He moved along the wall until he reached the nearest door. He opened it and slid through into the even deeper darkness beyond. Up above, at the top of the stairs, a faint light filtered beneath the other door which was his objective, the door that opened on to the upper regions of the Golden Wheel.

He began to climb the stairs and his feet made no sound because they were clad in moccasins, Indian-fashion. At the top he stopped and drew his gun. He waited and listened.

He heard slow pacing footsteps in the passage. They came nearer and the scent of tobacco-smoke drifted through to him. The footsteps came yet nearer then they stopped and the door behind which he stood creaked as if somebody had leaned against the other side. There was silence then, but the scent of smoke was much stronger.

Suddenly boot-heels scraped and the footsteps started up again and the man with the gun knew the other was going away again. Slowly he lifted the latch of the door and opened it.

As he stepped through, the smoking man's lean back was towards him. No sound startled him for he turned around slowly. Then his jaw dropped as he looked into the muzzle of the other's gun. The long scar on his cheek shone livid in the light as he said:

'The Kid.'

'Keep walking, Josh,' said Johnny Salom.

The other's face went deathly pale. He watched the Kid's eyes and something he saw in them made him tremble as he advanced slowly. Like a cornered rat his own eyes were shifty, his body was tensed as if to spring. Only panic could make such as he a brave man and he was very near to it now.

When he was only a few paces away from the levelled gun the man who held it said:

'Is Craig Jepson in his room?'

Josh licked dry lips. 'Yes, he's in there.'

'Where's your precious brother?'

'I think he's downstairs somewhere.'

'Reach your left hand across your belly, Josh, an' give me your gun.' As he spoke the Yaqui Kid let his own gun droop a little as if he despised Josh that much he could afford to take chances with him.

Josh's left hand crept across his belly. Then his right hand moved doubly swift in a desperate draw. Even as his hand closed over the butt of his gun the other man's weapon was descending and, looking suddenly into those cruel dark eyes, Josh knew that he had been tricked. He opened his mouth to yell but the sound died in his throat as the muzzle of the gun caught him squarely across the temple.

Johnny Salom caught him as he slumped, the blood already gushing from the wound. He opened a small door to the left of him and dragged the unconscious man into the lumber-hole and shut him in. He figured he'd sleep for a while. He might even die. But the Yaqui Kid saved his pity.

He moved fast along the passage, opened another door and stepped inside the lamplit room. He heard a gasp from the washroom on his left. Then there was a patter of feet and Annabella Strudel came through the curtains. She stood transfixed as if she could hardly believe her eyes when she saw him.

She wore a dressing-gown but it was open down the front and the figure-form of her spangled stage costume showed beneath. Her hand went up to her mouth in the old familiar gesture as he began to move towards her.

'I'm sorry, Annabella,' he said softly, 'that I acted as I did back in the cabin that mornin'. Can you forgive me?'

Something seemed to break within her. 'Johnny' she whispered and ran towards him.

She did not seem to realize that her robe was flying open. As he caught her his arms went instinctively inside it, clutching her slim body to his. It was a new feeling he experienced, an almost unbearable tenderness as he felt her trembling in his arms and heard her soft sobs as she pressed her face to his shoulder. The scent of her tawny hair was in his nostrils and his head was awhirl as he whispered little incoherent soothing words into her ear.

Finally she looked up into his face. Her eyes were glowing, there was a look in them that made the Yaqui Kid humble. He realized that if this was the end of the trail for him before he cashed in his checks he had found something beyond price, beyond contemplation. He felt suddenly very sad but when she put his own fears into words he hastened to reassure her.

'Don't you worry, honey. It's all fixed. Nothing's gonna happen to me.'

A sudden gust of feeling swept over him and he held her tighter. She got up on her tiptoes to reach him and he bent his head a little to kiss her.

When he let her go she sank shakily on to the bed. She said:

'Oh, I'm glad you found out. I'm glad you realized. I wouldn't do anything to hurt you. Mr Lemmings has told me all about you. I believe in you Johnny.' She held up her hands to him and he took them, standing looking down at her.

'I want to help you. What can I do to help?'

'You can help me a lot, honey,' he said. 'Your show will start soon, won't it?'

'Any time now. If I don't go soon they'll be sending somebody up to remind me. It's dangerous for you to stay here.'

'I know,' he said. From his pocket he took a large red

and white bandanna and handed it to her. 'Go down and carry on with your show as if nothing had happened but take this with you.' He bent and slipped the end of the bandanna beneath the bracelet on her wrist.

Her hands were on his as he did so. She was reluctant to let him go although she knew she must do so. He straightened up again and stood looking at her once more. There was a little smile on his face. He said:

'You were like that the first time I saw you.'

She was not ashamed to let him see her like this in the privacy of her room. In a moment she would go downstairs and let many men see her like this. But that would be different. This was different, very different, and it brought her no shame: she was only glad that it should be so. But her eyes revealed her surprise at the words he spoke and the way in which he spoke them.

'You saw my show?' she said.

'Yes, I saw your show. But that isn't the time I was talking about.'

She had known somehow that that was not the time he talking about but still she was puzzled.

He said: 'That same night when they were after me I hid in here. You came in.'

She flushed and smiled. 'What would you have done if you had caught me here,' he said, and she replied softly, 'I don't know.' Then:

'How did you get away?'

He told her of how she had been called away. 'What would you have done if I hadn't?' she said and this time it was his turn to say, 'I don't know.'

'What did you think about me then?' she said, her face still pink, her eyes shining.

'I thought you were the most beautiful thing I had ever seen.'

'What else did you think?'

'I don't know what else I thought,' he said quite truthfully. He caught hold of her hands and pulled her to her feet.

'Yes,' she said, coming out of her reverie. 'I must go. And you must go too. It is dangerous to stay here any longer.'

'I have some unfinished business,' he said. 'Go on down and carry that bandanna where it can be seen.' Swiftly he bent and kissed her once more. 'Go on,' he said.

'Take care, my love,' she said then she turned and ran to the door. She waved the bandanna on her wrist before she closed the door behind her.

Johnny Salom waited until her footsteps faded then he crossed to the door himself. He must get the moon-glow out of his eyes, his head out of the clouds; there was grim work to be done.

TWELVE

Annabella's route to the stage was a circumspect one, taking her around the back of the bar. The girls were already waiting for her in the wings and the small band on the dais was playing the opening number. The curtain began to open and she sent the girls on in front of her as she always did.

She looked through the corner of the curtain and surveyed the packed room.

She saw Slim, the Texan straw-boss, and his two pardners, Happy and Lem. They were by the door marked Private, leading to the office which Craig Jepson seldom used since the Yaqui Kid had broken in on him that first night.

That was not so long ago as it seemed Annabella reflected as her gaze travelled on around the room. The Texas cowboys seemed to be there in force and, as usual, they were propping the walls up all around.

At the bar she saw Marshal Lafe Cuthbertson, Inch Lemmings, Jebb Downs and Cracker, black-bearded Jake Cornfield, and fat Jasper Lynecote, the banker.

They were all strung out in a row, watching the girls on the stage. A few yards away from them lounged Ike Salter.

Annabella heard her cue and danced onto the stage waving the bandanna which Johnny had given her. The volume of clapping was much less than she was accustomed to, much less than she had received when she first came here. She noted that most of it came from the Texans and that little group of townspeople at the bar. Even as these latter clapped they began to move.

More than a few curious glances were thrown at them as they went through the crowd and began to climb the stairs. Marshal Cuthbertson and Jasper Lynecote seemed almost unwilling to do so but they were in front and the others jostled them and kept them moving.

Annabella danced on mechanically, her eyes on the little party. They vanished into the gloom above and she saw Ike Salter begin to climb the stairs in their wake. He was followed by Slim, the Texan, who caught him up almost at the top and seemed to be jostling him a little. Then they too vanished. She saw Happy and Lem stood at the bottom of the stairs now, one foot each on the bottom step, their thumbs hooked in their belts as they watched the room and the dancers.

But many eyes were straying away from the feminine loveliness on the stage. There was something in the air, the feeling was communicated from one to the other until it filled the room and was almost tangible. The good folk of Tucson wondered what was afoot. One of the barmen was the next to make for the stairs.

The two Texans closed in and blocked him. The barman said something and Happy shook his head mournfully. The barman tried to get past them. Happy put his hand on the man's chest and pushed him. At the same time Lem stretched out a leg. The barman went backwards over it and hit the floor with a crash that resounded above the music and the dancing.

Three men surged forward, one of them bellowing, 'What's the idea?'

They pulled up short as they were confronted by a pair of drawn guns.

Happy shook his head lugubriously. 'We didn't think we'd hafta do this,' he said.

The barman rose to his feet. 'Back up with the others, pardner,' said Lem. The scowling man joined his three friends.

The other barman suddenly took an interest in something under his bar. He straightened up when something hard was jabbed into his back. A cheeky-looking young cowpoke grinned down at him and said:

'Fetch that shotgun out, friend, so that everybody kin see it.'

Rather shakily the barman produced his weapon and it was taken gently from him. 'You'd better go around with the others, friend,' said the young man.

The crowd surged again and somebody said loudly: 'Them damn Texans are up to their tricks again.'

The cheeky-looking puncher vaulted up on the bar and sat there with the shotgun held laxly in front of him, so laxly that it looked like it would go off at any minute.

'Stop the music, professor,' he said.

The pianist obeyed with alacrity. The girls stopped dancing and there was sudden dead silence.

'Don't go away, girls,' said the young man with a cheeky grin. He was enjoying himself up there.

But his thunder was suddenly stolen by Lem who barked 'Listen to me, folks. The Law, together with a kind of committee composed of some o' the most prominent citizens of this fair town are concerned with some mighty important business upstairs an' don't wish to be disturbed. We didn't expect no reactions and neither did they so we'll ask yuh jest to be patient for a bit. I will add that if anybody else tries to get past us he's gonna get hurt – and, furthermore there's enough of us pesky cowhands here to handle the whole boilin' of yuh. Look at young Clem up there with that shotgun – I've seen him knock a hundred-yard picket fence down flat with one blast o' one o' them things . . .'

He paused and the townsfolk looked at the grinning Clem who bowed and patted the stock of his weapon as if he would dearly love to try it out. The townsfolk looked around them. All the walls were held up by silent cowhands with their thumbs in their belts. There were even a couple of them in front of the batwings.

Feet shuffled and there were sullen growls and a few cries of 'You can't get away with it' and phrases of similar nature. But nobody made a sudden movement.

'Start up the music again boys and let's get on with the dancin',' yelled Lem.

The pianist hit a jangling chord out of sheer nervousness, then from the middle of the bar-room a voice shouted 'Dancing. Yeh! – It's dancing that's causing all the trouble. I'll bet that red-headed hussy an' her precious Yaqui Kid have got somep'n to do with this shindig . . .'

'Lay off that piano again,' bawled Lem.

The instrument jangled once more then became silent. Up on the stage Annabella Strudel stood rigid, her face gone a little white. She felt every eye upon her and wanted desperately to turn and run. But she stood her ground.

Lem said: 'I'd like the skunk who made that remark to come forward an' apologize to the lady.'

There was no answer to this request. Lem shrugged, lifted up one hand, took off his hat and scratched his head. The next moment every Texan in the room had a gun in his hand. There was a fighting-man's grim smile on many of their faces.

A bunch of them began to close in a little. The ranks of the townsmen held. The air was electric with suspense, death hung over everything. One false move and there would be bloody massacre. These Texans played for high stakes and they didn't back down to anybody. They kept a-coming.

Sluggishly the ranks of the townsmen broke to let them through. In the silence, broken only by shuffling feet, a girl giggled shrilly, her nerves on the verge of breaking-point.

The small group of Texans moved in further. There was a scuffle and a deep voice said: 'Leggo of me!'

The ranks broke again, split apart by the hurtling body of a big red-headed man. He landed on his hands and knees in front of the stage. Two Texans bent over him, caught hold of a large red ear apiece and, in this wise, hauled him to his feet.

'Apologize to the lady,' said one.

The big man's reply was not audible but the loud 'Ouch' he gave at the heels of it was. He squirmed in the grip of the two Texans, both of whom were almost as big as he.

'I won't,' he said. 'I won't. Ow! Leggo of me . . .'

Even some of the townsfolk began to grin. It was good to see Bill the Bully getting some of his own medicine. 'Down on your knees, you worm,' said one of the Texans. 'Down on your knees an' beg the lady's pardon . . .'

'No – ouch. I won't!' But despite his protestations and his struggles Bill was slowly forced down once more.

One of the Texans spoke again and his voice had changed. The good-humoured note had gone from it. He meant business.

'You cur,' he said and drew his gun swiftly, slashing down with it. The gleaming barrel missed Bill's prominent nose by a hair's-breadth. He squealed again as if he had been hurt and this time there was real terror in his voice.

'What you need is a good pistol-whipping,' said the Texan. 'That'd knock some manners into yuh. An' that's what you'll get if you don't get down pronto an' say you're sorry.'

He raised his gun again menacingly. Bill gave a loud gulp and flopped down on his knees.

The Texan said: 'Repeat after me: I'm mighty sorry for what I said, Miss Strudel.'

'I'm mighty sorry for what I said, Miss Strudel,' said Bill in a strangled voice.

'I'm a big dim-witted jackass who talks through the back of his neck.'

'I'm a big . . .'

'Louder, man, louder. Let the folks hear yuh. Everybody admires a man who'll admit when he's in the wrong.'

There was laughter at this and it came from every quarter of the room.

Bill saw the swinging gun out of the corner of his eye and sang out in an artificial high-pitched voice

'I'm a dim-witted jackass who talks through the back of his neck.'

'Fine . . . I didn't mean what I said, Miss Strudel.'

Shrieking like a parrot Bill repeated this too.

'And I won't ever say anything like that agin.'

'An' I won't ever say nothin' like that agin,' said Bill in a high croak and he collapsed on the floor like a deflated balloon.

The two Texans bowed to Miss Strudel and she said:

'Thank you boys. His apology is accepted. Please let him go now.'

One of them prodded Bill with his foot. 'Git up, skunk, an' get back in the middle of the crowd, where we cain't see your ugly mug.'

Bill rose and shambled away. One of the Texans lifted the big man's gun before he went. Even a craven bully like him was liable to turn nasty after the humiliation to which he had been subjected.

Lem yelled, 'Carry on with the music an' the dancin'. Let everybody be happy . . .'

The band struck up like a trio of nervous cats with cans on their tails but, grateful to be doing something to alleviate the nervous tension, soon got into their stride.

Annabella Strudel gave her girls their cue and they began. She danced with them mechanically, her eyes on the stairs all the time, wondering what was happening in the quietness of the gloom up there. And she reflected that never had she danced in such strange and perilous circumstances before and she hoped she never would again. If only she knew what was happening to Johnny . . . Johnny . . .

2

When Johnny Salom closed Annabella's door behind him and stood in the passage all was silent around him. He heard the music start up downstairs and knew that it was time for him to move.

He crossed the passage diagonally, soundlessly on his moccasined feet. He stopped outside another door, pressed his ear to the panel and listened. Slowly he pressed down the latch. Then with a quick movement he flung the door open.

Craig Jepson leapt up from his chair, reaching for the gun at his elbow. But the Yaqui Kid already had him covered. He kicked the door to behind him and came further into the room.

Jepson's face went white. He looked like a man at the end of his tether. He clasped his hands in front of him to stop them fluttering, to let the kid know that he didn't mean to make any funny movements. He clasped his left hand over his still bulky bandaged right one. His gun was on the table at his left-hand side and he knew he hadn't an earthly chance of getting it before the other man plugged him.

And he knew by the look in the other's dark eyes that he would kill him without hesitation. Shoot him in the stomach maybe and be delighted to watch him squirm and scream in agony. There was something cruel and implacable, very Indian-like about the Yaqui Kid's smooth mahogany face.

'What do you want?' said Jepson huskily.

'What do I want?' echoed the other. 'I want to hear a lot of things from you. I know the things I want to hear and I mean to hear them all before I leave this room. Whether you are alive or not when I leave here depends on how you tell those things . . .'

'I don't know what you're talking about.'

'Shut up,' said Johnny Salom. 'Don't say anythin' until you can say somep'n sensible. I'll tell you when to start talkin'. Put your hands above your head!'

Slowly, trying hard to dispel their trembling Jepson raised his hands. He realized he must pull himself together. He didn't know what was the matter with himself lately – letting a skunk like this get on his nerves. That was what the young devil had planned no doubt . . . But he'd show him yet. He'd bide his time, do as he was told. His chance would come . . .

The Yaqui Kid walked nearer, reached out with his free hand, and took the gun from the table and tucked it into his belt.

'Sit down,' he said. 'Then turn around and put your hands on the table.'

Jepson sat down. He even permitted himself a slight smile as he did as he was told.

'Get on with your business,' he said. 'What are these things you want to know?'

'I'll begin by telling you a story,' said Johnny Salom. 'Then I'll ask questions and, by God, you'd better answer them properly.' His sudden flash of fury contorted his face for a moment and Jepson almost recoiled as he saw a devil shining there. But he tried to appear amused as he said:

'All right. Go on with your story.'

'I'll be as brief as possible,' said Johnny Salom. 'It all starts with an old-timer named Lijah Pentecost. He was a prospector who liked to work alone an' he'd been looking for gold in these parts for nigh on twenty years. He panned dust now an' then which kept him in vittles, but very often he was flat broke. Many's the time my mother grub-staked him. I guess she was the best friend the old cuss had got.

'Then one day the old man found a bonanza. He told everybody about it but naturally he did not tell them where it was. Most of the townsfolk didn't believe him anyway. He'd come with the same tale so many times before. My mother was the only person he trusted with his full secret. He even gave her a map to keep for him and promised her a share when he made his big haul . . .'

'I remember Lijah,' said Jepson. 'He left these parts before you were put in gaol – I can't see what he has to do with me . . .'

Johnny Salom said: 'You remember him do you? If so mebbe you'll remember that he was very fond of whiskey. You might also remember how two prospector friends of yours plied him with whiskey one night downstairs in your office which they had *borrowed* for the occasion. Lijah wanted somebody to help him with his claim, these seemed two nice fellers, before he knew where he was the drunken old sot was asking them to come and work with him. It was very early when the three of them left town the following morning. I guess that I, who was always snooping around when everybody else was in bed, was the only person who saw them go. Whether they saw me or not I don't know. In the light of what happened later I guess one of them did.

'That was the last I saw of Lijah Pentecost. It was the last anybody in this territory saw of him in fact. It was thought that he had gone bust again and moved to pastures new. The two prospectors appeared in town again. What had happened between them and the old man out in the badlands I do not know. Maybe he turned suspicious. Mebbe there was a fight and they killed him. Mebbe they tortured him to make him tell. He didn't tell but in some way they must've learnt that my mother knew his secret. I presume that through it all, being your boys they kept in touch with you.'

'It all sounds like a fairy tale to me,' said Jepson.

'Does it? Well, listen to this. One morning those two prospector friends paid a visit to my mother's cabin.

144

She was out and they searched it. They found nothing of interest. I saw them come out, stopped them by the creek and challenged them. They threw down on me. You know the rest. I killed them both. One of them, firing wildly as he fell, plugged his own pardner in the side. That slug, with plenty of help from you, sent me right along for fifteen years in the State Pen. There were no witnesses but it was alleged that I shot them down from ambush. Otherwise, how did that man come to have a bullet in his side? Of course, me being Johnny Salom, the outcast Yaqui Kid, very few people believed my story. The few that tried to help me never stood a chance. No more than I did . . .'

'You were tried fairly in a court of law.'

'Fairly hell! Your damn marshal, your damn judge. . . ! What did happen to the marshal by the way? He left the county pretty hurriedly I'm told. Was he pushed by you? I bet you were sorry you let him go afterwards though, weren't you? The one you've got here now is a different proposition. You can't buy him. . . ! Don't make me lose my temper, Craig. I want to get on with my story.'

Jepson shrugged, trying to appear insolently at ease. The cold killer-light in Johnny Salom's eyes now was as bad as anything that flared there when he lost his temper!

The Kid went on unemotionally. 'You waited till I was safely in gaol then you got to work on my mother. What you did to her I don't know but finally you got hold of the map. Then you had her killed – by the simple process of holding her head under water until she

145

drowned. It looked like suicide.' He leaned forward. 'Over and over again I've told myself what I'd do to you when I caught you. Kill you slowly and laugh while I watched you die. But to do that won't bring my mother back. And it won't help me – only brand me for all time as an outlaw killer. So I'm gonna turn you over to the law and let them hear your story . . .'

'Don't be a fool,' said Jepson and he almost grinned. Hope was returning to him once more.

The other man carried on as if he had not spoken. He leaned nearer. 'I want that map,' he said. 'The map of Lijah Pentecost's claim. The map of the mine you've just closed down after milking it dry.'

'I haven't got any map,' said Jepson.

Johnny Salom's white teeth were suddenly bared. The gun flashed in his hand and the barrel came down with terrific force on the bandaged hand lying on the table-top.

Jepson screamed shrilly with surprise and terrible agony, his body stiffening in his chair, his head thrown back. The smashed hand remained spread on the table-top and blood began to seep sluggishly through the white bandages.

Jepson's face was dead-white, his eyes rolled with pain as he swayed in the chair. He saw the dark, satyr-like face of Johnny Salom looming above him. The thin cruel lips opened and the voice said:

'I want that map, Craig. You'd better get it for me. How should you like your other hand smashed to match? Or your face cut to ribbons by the sight of this gun just like I slashed the ugly mug of your pal, Josh.'

Mention of Josh made the saloon-owner realize how much he was at this devil's mercy. Even if anybody came to his rescue the Kid could kill him before they had a chance to do anything.

'I'll get the map,' he said weakly. 'It's in my desk.'

Johnny Salom stood away from him. 'All right,' he said. 'Take it easy.'

Jepson rose shakily and braced himself then he skirted the table and began to cross slowly to the tall roll-top desk in the corner of the room. He was a desperate man now, far more desperate than he looked. He glanced back over his shoulder and was surprised at what he saw.

Johnny Salom had put his gun down on the table, had produced his makings and was rolling himself a quirly. Doubtless he thought that, as his captive hadn't got a gun, and only one hand he couldn't do any harm nohow. And in any case, so fast was the Kid, that he could grab that gun off the table quicker than batting an eyelash if the saloon-man made any funny moves.

With his left hand Jepson hooked the key from off the wall behind the desk. He inserted it in the lock and opened the desk. All the time he was watching the Kid's movements through the convenient glass front of a small bookcase beside the desk.

As Johnny Salom licked the cigarette paper he held it in both hands to finish off his job neatly. Jepson rummaged in his desk, found what he sought and turned with it in his hand.

'All right, Johnny,' he said. 'Keep your hands right where they are.'

The expression on the Yaqui Kid's usually immobile face was ludicrous, as he looked into the mouth of a Colt. His cigarette remained motionless in his hands, his mouth open in the process of licking the paper.

'Smart but not quite smart enough,' said Craig Jepson. 'The map's here behind me. As soon as I've shot you – in self-defence – I'm going to burn it. You were right in everything you said though it isn't of any use to you to know that now. Two of my men killed your mother after they'd made her give them the map. Get ready to join her, Johnny.'

His finger whitened on the trigger. He did not see the bedroom door beside him open. But he saw Johnny's eyes flicker in that direction. Then a voice barked: 'Drop it, Jepson!'

He turned and confronted the guns of Inch Lemmings and the marshal. Then he went to pieces. The Colt dropped from his hand and he staggered back, half-fainting, against the bookcase.

THIRTEEN

Johnny Salom blew out a gusty sigh of relief.

'I wanted him to pull a trick like that,' he said. 'But I didn't expect you *hombres* to cut it so fine.'

'I had him covered all the time,' said Inch Lemmings. Behind the two men filed Jeb Downs and Cracker, Jake Cornfield and Jasper Lynecote.

'There are plenty of witnesses here,' said the marshal. 'An' they heard it all. It looks like a clean bill of health to you, son, from now on, an' I'm mighty glad to hear it.'

Johnny Salom sat down in the chair vacated by the saloon-owner.

'That's the first time anybody's said anythin' like that to me,' he said, almost to himself. 'It shore feels good.' He looked up and his eyes caught those of fat Jasper Lynecote. 'My apologies are due to you, sir,' he said with a little bow.

'Forget it, son,' boomed the banker. 'It was worth it to see this snake showed up for what he is.'

'Wal, I guess we'd better get him downstairs,' said the

149

marshal, 'an' let all the folks know what's what.' He caught hold of the drooping saloon-owner's arm. 'Come on, yuh skunk, move!'

Johnny Salom strode up to the desk and picked something up from there. It was a tattered dirty piece of paper with lines and marks on it like the scribble of a child.

'Lijah Pentecost's map,' he said. 'What a lot of grief it caused ... Wal, I guess it ain't no more good to nobody now.'

He held it up, preparatory to tearing it.

'Give it to me,' said the marshal taking it from him. 'It's evidence.'

The cavalcade moved out into the passage. There they discovered Slim squatting with his back to the wall and smoking an evil-smelling cheroot. Sprawled on his back nearby, his mouth wide-open and his eyes closed was Ike Salter.

'He fell an' hit his head,' said Slim. 'He ain't daid. He's jest havin' a nice long sleep.'

'I'll send somebody up to collect him,' said the marshal. 'Thanks for everything, Slim,' said Johnny Salom as the lanky straw-boss rose.

'Wouldn't've missed it for worlds,' said Slim. 'Wal, I guess I'd better come down an' see how my boys are getting on.'

As the cavalcade began to descend the stairs the music was still playing and the girls were still dancing. Then all heads turned and an excited babble rose. The band stopped playing, the girls stopped dancing, the Texans holstered their guns and rested their weary arms.

'They've got the Yaqui Kid!' yelled somebody.

'Look at Jepson,' bawled somebody else. 'What's the matter with him?'

Marshal Cuthbertson raised his hands before his head. 'Quiet, you monkeys,' he bawled. 'Quiet.'

Slowly, the babble died to a sullen murmur. The marshal opened his mouth to speak again but he was not destined to do so right then.

A girl's voice from the stage yelled shrilly 'Look out!' and a man appeared from the gloom at the top of the stairs. He was swaying, a gun in each hand and his face was hideous with blood. The party on the stairs scattered as the guns began to flame.

The Yaqui Kid's draw was the fastest of all. As he threw himself forward he was fanning the hammer of his gun, sending a stream of lead screaming up the stairs at the bloodied, half-crazy Josh Salter.

The slugs intended for the Kid whined over his head. They thunked into something behind him and he heard a thin scream and somebody say 'God' softly. Then Josh Salter, almost cut in half by a hail of lead, began to fall. The men crouched against the side of the stairs as the body came hurtling down.

But there were two bodies that came to rest at the bottom. The other one belonged to Craig Jepson. Wretched and bemused he had not got out of the line of fire in time and slugs from the guns of his own hireling had riddled him.

Happy and Lem bent over the two bodies. Happy looked up. His face was a picture of misery. 'They're both purty daid,' he said.

There was a thunder of hoofs from outside and a man tumbled, wild-eyed, through the batwings yelling:

'Injuns! Injuns! The place is alive with 'em.'

For a moment the room was a study in astonishment and suspended animation. Then there was a general movement towards the door. Even the Yaqui Kid was forgotten in the excitement of this new development.

The batwings swung open again and three be-feathered Yaqui chiefs came in. The moving white men stopped. Everything hung on a hair-trigger. Then the Yaqui Kid drew attention to himself once more by shouting:

'Hold it everybody.'

All eyes, including those of the warriors were turned towards him.

He spoke again, in guttural Indian dialect and the three Yaquis raised their hands in salute. They turned and jabbered to each other, making signs in the Kid's direction.

He began to descend the stairs. 'Let him through, yuh monkeys,' bawled Marshal Cuthbertson. 'He's cleared. He's free. Craig Jepson's the one you've got to thank for all your grief.'

The crowd parted in waves and Johnny Salom went through them and joined his Indian friends at the door. He spoke to them once more. Then he turned to the marshal and the rest, who had left the stairs and were advancing across the floor.

'They came to see if I needed any help,' he said. 'I have assured them that I am free and unharmed and they are prepared to return to their village if I will go back with them to see the chief, who is too old to ride.'

He turned then and passed through the batwings with the three braves. Everybody else surged after them and gasped at the sight that met their eyes.

The street was packed from sidewalk to sidewalk with mounted red men. As the Kid and his escort came out a ripple ran through their ranks and there was a collective guttural grunt.

One of the chiefs raised his arms above his head and spoke, resting his hand lightly on Johnny Salom's shoulder as he did so.

There was silence until he had finished then another rumbling, guttural grunt. But there was something a little different about it this time.

Bronzed, muscular bodies gleamed in the lights that were going on all around. There was a forest of tall painted lances and gently waving feathers. Many of the naked torsoes were daubed with paint to match the hideous mask of their faces. Many a white man's hand clutched his gun as he watched and waited.

An Indian came along leading a horse. It was Johnny Salom's own paint pony. Others brought the three horses belonging to the chiefs. The four men mounted, then solemnly rode to the head of the cavalcade.

One of the chiefs gave a shrill cry and made a sweeping forward movement with his hand. Slowly the sluggish gleaming mass of muscular human flesh and smooth horseflesh began to move. It gathered speed as it went down the street and the last the townspeople saw of Johnny Salom was a wave of his gloved hand.

'Gosh,' said Inch Lemmings. 'It's a good thing for

Tucson that the Yaqui Kid did pull off his hat-trick up in that room tonight.'

Just behind him a lovely red-headed girl with a dressing gown wrapped around her looked out into the night, out to the soft pulse of the fading hoofs. Her eyes gleamed with tears as the light caught them.

EPILOGUE

Although it was broad daylight nobody saw the lean young man climb the fence at the side of the Golden Wheel. He dropped into the alley, slid along the wall to the door, opened it and passed through. He climbed the backstairs on moccasined feet, opened the other door and went into the passage. He crept along to the second door on the right-hand side of the passage, opened that and went into the room.

The girl by the bed had her back to him. She turned with a little cry of alarm, her hand flying up to her mouth.

'Hallo, Annabella,' he said.

'Hallo,' she said almost inaudibly, and turned her back on him once more.

He leaned against the door and studied her. She wore a shapely plum-coloured travelling outfit with a little bustle. Perched sideways on the gleaming wealth of her hair was a perky little green hat. The young man did not know much about women's clothes but he figured she looked dandy. He took his sombrero off quickly, rather sheepishly and rolled it around in his hands.

Before the girl on the bed was an open travelling case. All around her were articles of feminine attire. She crammed these swiftly, nervously, into the interior of the case with obviously no thought to space or arrangement. She turned suddenly and crossed to the dressing-table. She opened a drawer and from there took more flimsy articles. She rolled them up in a ball, hiding them against her side out of the sight of the young man as she carried them back to the case. She did not look at him. Her face was set, her lids lowered.

'Goin' someplace?' said the young man in a brightly conversational tone.

'Yes.' The reply was terse, uncompromising.

'Where?'

'Back East.'

'Do you like it back East?'

'Yes. It's my proper home.'

'Is it? Have you got any particular reason for goin' back there? Any *really* particular reason for goin' back there?'

'I've got friends back there.'

'Friends? What friends?'

She turned on him then, her full lower lip caught between her teeth. 'I've got friends,' she hissed. 'I don't have to stay here.' She turned back to her packing.

'Leaving the troupe?' he said.

' Yes.'

'Goin' back East all alone?'

'Well, if it's any business of yours, yes, I am going alone. I can look after myself.'

'Hey, you haven't got a husband waiting for you back there have you?'

'No.'

'Cain't see any sense in goin' back there if you haven't got a husband waitin' for yuh.' The young man paused. He seemed to be chewing ruminatively. The girl threw a balled-up garment into the case with unnecessary violence. At length the young man said:

'Now if you were to stay out West I'd venture to wager you'd get yourself a husband pretty easily. Kinda quickly too I guess, a purty girl like you.'

She turned then to face him. 'Do you really think so, Johnny?' she said.

'Doggone it, yes,' he said, moving away from the door. 'Sure.'

He held out his arms and she ran into them. He said: 'You catching the stage?'

'I was,' she said.

'Go ahead and catch it,' he said.

Pain shot into her eyes and she tried to push him away from her. He laughed.

'Easy, yuh little vixen,' he said. 'You gotta get used to having me around. I'm catching that stage myself.'

'You are?'

'Yeh, sure. You didn't think I meant to stay around here did yuh? I'm looking for a small-holding someplace else, a gel, a friendly preacher . . .'

What else he meant to say was unknown for his mouth was closed suddenly by her soft lips.

Afterwards she said: 'But your stuff? Your luggage? Where is it?'

'It's already in the stage,' he said. 'I stopped it back along the trail an' fixed everything then I came on ahead to pick up you.'

'Pretty sure of yourself weren't you, Johnny Salom?'

'Yeh,' he said. 'I guess so . . . Hey, there it is! Shut that portmanteau up, honey, and come on.'

When they got out on the sidewalk Inch Lemmings was standing there. With him were Slim, Happy and Lem.

'Here come the happy couple,' said the latter.

Johnny Salom grinned and went past them to put the big case on the stage. He turned at a touch on his arm. It was Slim.

The Texan said: 'Where yuh bound for, *amigo*?'

'No place in particular; a patch of grass under the sky, a cabin, a preacher to call.'

'Is it a job you want?'

'Mebbe.'

'I've got one for yuh if you'll come back to Texas with me. The old man can always use new hands. I've already signed up your pard, Inch.'

'That's right,' grinned the blocky red-head.

'What do you say, Johnny?' said Slim. 'You kin get married up there. There's plenty of room for you an' Annabella. It's young, beautiful country.'

The young man looked at his bride-to-be. She nodded, her eyes shining.

Johnny Salom held out his hand to Slim. 'From now on I'm a cowhand,' he said.

Author's Note

The description of Indian dancing in this story is authentic. Such traditional ceremonies are still carried on to this day, almost unchanged, by the remaining Yagui Indians on their reservations on the edge of the Arizona 'badlands'.

V.J.H.